Dec. 2019

For Sue —
My dear friend ♥ I miss
seeing you all in the neighborhood.
Hope to see you all soon ♥

Love,
Sandy

MONEY MAN

MAROONED

Sandra M Bush

Sᴀɴᴅʀᴀ M. Bᴜѕʜ

Year of the Book
135 Glen Avenue
Glen Rock, PA 17327

Print ISBN: 978-1-64649-022-6
eBook ISBN: 978-1-64649-023-3

Library of Congress Control Number: 2019914139

DEDICATION

With love for my family:
Todd, Chelsea, and Monica.
The people who make me laugh
every day.

ACKNOWLEDGMENTS

With many thanks and great appreciation to:

Demi Stevens, my magical editor and friend.
My Rebel Writer Critique Companions Cindy and Jeanne.
My Pennwriters friends who remind me to write every day.
My readers who encouraged me to write my sequel.

CHAPTER 1

Sweat streamed off Tom Frye from every pore in his body, and the late afternoon summer sun seared his face. Now he remembered why he'd hated manual labor as a young man. No one had ever claimed trimming Christmas trees was glamorous work. But when he bought the Country Bumpkin five years ago, he vowed to do any job he expected an employee to perform. Considerable gray flecked his dark hair, and the increased time spent outdoors added a rugged, weathered appearance to his face. He wiped his brow with the bandana in his shorts' pocket and kept working. Tom stretched his tall, lean body and groaned. His arms and shoulders ached with fatigue, and he had another six hours left to work.

The irony of his situation infuriated him. *Be careful what you wish for, Tom. You had to leave your job as a financial advisor to buy a landscaping company. Serves you right. Suck it up.*

He sighed, grabbed the shears from the wheelbarrow, and climbed back up the ladder. Those trees hadn't gotten the attention they deserved last year, and they'd grown tall and gangly. Hardly the perfect Christmas tree shape the public expected.

Walter, his right-hand employee, had been on vacation that week, so Tom tackled the job solo. Getting the business up and running had been harder than he thought. But with Walter's help, they'd get those trees in shape before the end of the summer.

A rustling sound under a neighboring pine caught his attention. He climbed down the ladder and followed the noise to find a black mother cat and her litter of a half-dozen mewling offspring. Varied in color, the kittens curled against their mother and nursed. Intrigued, and despite his dislike for cats, Tom wanted a closer look.

Great, another problem to deal with. Feral cats taking over the place. I hate to admit it, but they're pretty cute.

He inched closer. At first the mother cat ignored him, tending to her brood, but after a few moments, she glared at Tom, challenging him to keep his distance. Her green eyes bored into him, steady and protecting. Tom couldn't help himself, moving closer. He couldn't remember ever seeing a mother cat with such young kittens outdoors like that.

For a few moments, he stood nearby, watching them. The mother cat relaxed and snuggled against her babies, so he crept even closer and crouched next to her. A bright pink collar was visible against the lush black fur around her neck, with a large pet ID tag. He moved a few steps nearer to see if he could read it. Yep, there in large, bold letters, the tag identified the mother cat as "Kitty."

Oh, good. It's someone's pet. That's a relief. Not a very creative name, though. Overcome with an unexplainable urge, and close enough now to touch her, Tom reached down to pet the top of the cat's head and scratched behind her ears. At first, Kitty craned her neck in appreciation, luxuriating in the attention... then chomped down on Tom's right hand. Hard.

"Ouch! Ooh. Jesus H. Christ." The cat held fast with her sharp teeth, biting harder into the tender web of flesh between his thumb and forefinger. "Let go, dammit!"

After a full thirty seconds, the cat released Tom's hand and began to hiss. She arched her back and lifted a paw to swat in case Tom decided to go in for another round.

Tom backed away from the cats and looked at his hand. Two neat puncture wounds pierced his flesh and trickled blood.

"Well, this is great!" Tom screamed to no one. "How could I be so stupid?" He pulled a red handkerchief from his back pocket and wound it around his hand to protect it.

Gathering his tools, Tom threw them into the wheelbarrow and walked back to the store. As he steered around the potholes in the service road, he tried to protect his injured hand from its rough wooden handle.

Tom saw Vicky chatting with one of their regular customers at the rose display in front of the store. He marveled at his wife's ability to talk to anyone with great ease. He watched her dark ponytail bobbing up and down while she flashed her magazine smile. She loved people and thrived when surrounded with customers needing help. *Vicky would've made a better broker than me. She's certainly a lot prettier.*

Yet, Tom didn't second-guess his decision to leave his job as a financial advisor. He'd left at the top of his game. Leaving that job remained the best decision he ever made, except for marrying Vicky. Still, it got under his skin when his ex-business partner Lance popped into the Country Bumpkin every so often, blathering about his booming business. Those days, the old familiar pang of competition stabbed his ego.

Tom stood off to the side of the entrance while Vicky continued chatting with a little old lady. When she caught his eye, he motioned her to come over.

"Hey there, honey. What's up with the bandage? Did you hurt yourself?"

"I was attacked." Tom waved his wrapped hand in the air. "By a wild animal." He watched his wife and waited for a response.

"What? Oh my God! What happened?" She lowered her voice and leaned in closer. "It wasn't a bird, was it?" Reaching for his hand, she tried to examine the injury.

Tom snorted. "No. It wasn't a bird." Leave it to Vicky to remind him of the time he'd faced off against dive-bombing birds while mowing the lawn. He pulled his hand out of her reach. "It was a cat—some crazed, black cat. It attacked me."

"A cat? But I thought you were trimming Christmas trees? Was it feral, do you think? Hiding in the trees?" Vicky's gaze penetrated his, pushing for details. "What happened?"

"Well, I was up on the hill, trimming the trees when I heard strange noises. I got off the ladder to investigate and came across a mother cat and her litter of kittens hidden in the pine needles. I guess I got a little too close and she attacked me."

"You got too close? What does that mean? Did you try to touch the kittens?" Typical Vicky. She'd chosen to side with the beast over him.

"No. Of course I did not touch the kittens."

"So what—"

Tom interrupted, deciding he might as well spill the beans. "I petted the mother cat, and Vick, she liked it. She did! Then, all of a sudden, she attacked me. Didn't let go either, for like a minute." He started to remove the bandage to show her the wound, when she chastised him.

"What in God's name is wrong with you? You can't go up to a strange cat and pet it. Not one that's just had kittens. Why would you do something so stupid?"

"I don't know. But I need to figure out who owns that cat. What if it hasn't had its shots?" His eyes grew wild and he turned and grabbed her by the shoulders. "Vick, what if it has rabies, or something worse? I've gotta find that cat."

"All right, but let's clean that bite off first." She peered at the puncture wound, which looked more red and swollen by the minute. Taking him by the hand, she pulled him into the store's office bathroom and got the first-aid kit.

After she cleaned and bandaged the wound, Tom persuaded Vicky to help him find the black cat. They trudged up the hill to the Christmas tree farm and looked around.

"Okay, so where'd you leave off with your trimming? Do you remember?"

Tom slapped his head and then winced at the pain from his palm. "Oh, man. I bet I forgot to leave a flag where I left off."

Vicky turned to face him and threw him a dirty look. "Well think, Tom. Shouldn't you be able to tell which trees have been trimmed?" But the look on his face as they scanned row after row of trees spoke volumes.

"Give me a minute. Don't have kittens." He shrugged his shoulders and mumbled, "Sorry."

"Tom, I'm roasting to death out here. For God's sake, think. Concentrate. What kind of landmarks do you remember? Any odd looking trees? Old stumps? Anything?" Vicky blew out a big breath and wiped sweat off the back of her neck with her hand. "Gross."

Tom ignored his wife and trudged along the rows of pines, hoping something would jog his memory. Then, he remembered. The ladder. He'd left it at the tree he worked on last.

"Okay, I think I may have left the ladder there. I couldn't quite reach without it. And I don't remember throwing it on the wheelbarrow. It should be there."

"Well, that's good," said Vicky. "All we need to do is find the ladder."

They continued walking until they eventually spotted it, leaning against a tree with a ragged top.

"There it is! Okay, now all we need to do is find the cat and those kittens."

They searched all around the tree, but neither of them saw the cat or her babies.

Vicky huffed and put her hands on her hips. "Well, no cat. Or kittens. She must've moved them after you disturbed her."

"I didn't disturb them, Vick, all I did was pet the damn cat."

"Like I said, you disturbed the mother. That cat wasn't taking any chances in case you came back. They do that, you know. Move their babies if they're in danger from predators."

"Boy, you're just hilarious, aren't you?" Tom raged. "Vicky, I need to find that cat and make sure it's had its shots."

"Tom, I am not going to spend the entire afternoon—especially in this heat—looking for some mysterious cat creature that attacked you. I have all of those roses to re-pot back at the store." She turned and started walking. "I'm leaving. I'll talk to you later."

Angry and frustrated, Tom watched her walk away. He searched a bit on his own, but didn't have any luck. He looked all around the area, but Kitty had vanished. He decided he'd have to give up and go back to the store too, so he made his way to the service road. That's when he saw the flash of black watching him from the tall grass.

"Aha, there you are. Come here, you little bitch. Here kitty, kitty, kitty." He took a few tentative steps in the direction of the cat, which remained partially hidden by the high grass.

All I need to do is get close enough to see what's on that pink collar. And I need to grab it so it can't bite me again. Somewhere in his mind he heard Vicky's voice telling him to stay away from stray animals. But he continued moving toward the mother cat, until the unthinkable happened. The cat started moving toward him, meowing, and then ran right up to him and plopped down at his toes. It rubbed up against his legs, weaving in between his feet. Tom could hear it purring. Yes, it was a beautiful black cat. But it wasn't wearing a pink collar. This wasn't Kitty.

He petted the cat tentatively, but it showed no fear. Quite the opposite, this cat loved the attention. Definitely not the same cat. No way. Stumped, Tom turned and continued down the road toward the store. The new cat watched him walk away, arched its back in a stretch and trotted back off into the weeds.

Bewildered, Tom tried not to overreact, but he couldn't help himself. If he told Vicky he'd discovered another cat, a friendly one, after the first cat had bitten him, she'd think he'd gone crazy. He needed to convince his family to help him keep looking for the original culprit.

After they finished their supper, Tom persuaded Vicky and the girls to return to the tree farm to look for his attacker. He decided to keep mum about the second feline. They took a flashlight looking for the mother cat, but got only mosquito bites for their trouble. An exhaustive search of the tree farm and the grounds of the Country Bumpkin produced no black cat with a pink collar. The other mysterious and friendly black cat Tom encountered remained elusive as well.

"Tom, there's no sign of Kitty," Vicky said. "The girls and I have combed every inch of this farm and we can't find a trace of any cats. Black or otherwise." She walked over and put her arm around eighteen-year-old Sophie, planting a kiss on top of her blonde head. "We need to get home. It's too dark to see anything." Vicky shivered. "Besides, it's creepy out here. Let's go."

"Yeah, Daddy. I need to get home and start packing. I leave for college again in two weeks!" Sophie left her mother's embrace and walked to stand next to her father. "Dad? Hello?" Her green eyes peered into his dark gaze.

"Yes, fine. Go then." Tom paced in a circle and shooed her away. "Skat!" He winced and pulled off his Orioles cap, turning it over and over in his hands. "Sorry. No more cat jokes. I guess I'm destined for rabies shots."

Jane walked up the path to rejoin her parents and sister. "Any luck?"

"Nope. No sign of any black cats anywhere. I'm screwed." Tom continued to pace and wring his hat in his hands.

Jane tried one last attempt at luring in the feline mother, shaking the can of Pounce cat treats she'd brought along for bait. "Dad, wait and see what the doctor says tomorrow," she reasoned. "Be optimistic."

"Optimistic, my ass, Jane. Easy for you to say."

Sassy, red-headed Jane turned toward her mother and sister and made the rolling finger next to her head signal, universally recognized as indicating a crazy person.

"I saw that. Not funny."

"Not trying to be funny, Dad."

"Fine. Then you're grounded."

"Dad, I'm twenty-three. I'm too old for grounding." Jane stifled a laugh. "Besides, I barely live here anymore."

Tom scowled and trudged toward the car. Pulling out his cell as he walked, he scrolled his contacts until he found what he needed. After keying in the appropriate prompts, he heard a human voice answer his call.

"Hello? Answering service? Yes, hi, this is Tom Frye. A stray animal has bitten me, and I think I'd better come in and see the doctor. Yes. Thanks, I'll see you tomorrow morning."

CHAPTER 2

Tom slept fitfully that night, imagining he'd wake up foaming at the mouth and trying to bite his family. When he rolled out of bed the next morning, he staggered to the bathroom and ripped off the bandage. His hand looked infected and sore. The two pronounced puncture marks, bright red and swollen, now oozed yellow pus.

He grabbed the sink, fearing he would faint. His heart pounded so hard, he thought it might burst through his chest, so he sat on the toilet seat and tried to gain control. *Everything will be fine. My doctor's appointment is at 8:45. They'll help me.*

He managed a quick shower and shave and made it downstairs. Vicky rose and greeted him with a cup of coffee and a peck on the cheek.

"Hey, hon. How's the hand? Better today?" She craned her neck to try to get a look, but he hid it protectively under his armpit.

"No. It's worse! Looks awful." He slurped a sip of coffee and winced as it scalded his lips.

"Oh, no. Let's see?" Vicky tried to pry his hand from under his armpit, but he resisted, backing away.

"No. I'll wait for the doctor to check it out." Tom sat at the table, sipped his coffee again and pretended to look at the newspaper. "So, you're opening the store today? Right?"

"I don't need to open. Walter is coming back from vacation today, thank God. Don't you want me to drive you to your appointment?"

Tom peered over his newspaper. "Okay, I guess." He'd expected to go to the doctor alone. Sometimes Vicky's hovering made him more anxious. But his hand felt too sore to drive anyway.

After he forced down a few morsels of breakfast, they climbed in the car. As Vicky drove, she chattered on about Sophie needing to pack for her junior year of college, and hiring some extra help at the store after all the high school and college kids left at the end of the summer.

He struggled to pay attention, but his imagination was no match for Vicky's small talk. Tom recalled the horror stories he'd heard about humans needing rabies shots. A series of painful injections, he thought. *I think they give you those shots in your stomach.* He imagined the sharp needles poking through his abdomen and accidentally pricking some vital organ, like his liver. He struggled not to vomit in the car.

When he walked through the doors into the doctor's office, Tom's queasiness increased. *Oh, no. That's one of the symptoms, right?* He struggled to remember what he'd researched on the web the night before. The CDC claimed early signs of rabies included flu-like symptoms, general weakness or discomfort, fever, headache. He touched his forehead to gauge his temperature, and sat in the closest seat available.

"Tom?" Vicky looked perplexed. "Check in with the receptionist."

"What? Oh yeah." He walked toward reception wiping his damp forehead.

"Sir, can I help you?" the young woman at the desk inquired. "Name?"

"Frye. Tom Frye."

"Hi, Tom," the young woman said handing over a clipboard with papers and a pen attached by a string. "Could you fill these out, please? So we can update our files?" She smiled.

Tom noticed her nose had a tiny diamond stud in the left nostril. His mind whirred. *Left side. Does that mean she's gay? Not that it matters... Maybe that's only for men with earrings?* He shook his head back and forth to clear his mind.

"What did you say?" Tom looked to the woman for clarification.

"You haven't been here for a while. It's time to update your records. Do you have your current insurance card? And you'll need to fill out these forms and sign at the bottom."

Tom spun around and looked at Vicky. He raised an eyebrow and nodded his head in the direction of the receptionist.

"Vick?"

"Tom, take the clipboard. Complete the forms," Vicky said, rolling her eyes. She rummaged in her purse and handed the insurance card to the receptionist. "Here you go. Thanks." Vicky grabbed Tom's arm and pulled him to a chair while the receptionist copied their insurance card.

"What a pain in the ass. Why do they need to know all this?" Tom flipped through the pages. "Look! Three different forms. Don't they have this stuff on file? We've been coming here forever. And my hand hurts too much."

"Tom," Vicky hissed under her breath. "You're making a scene." She leaned closer to him and grabbed the clipboard. "Here. Give them to me. I'll fill them out."

He blew out a big breath and watched as Vicky scrawled through the forms. When completed, she thrust them into his lap. Tom carried the paperwork to the young woman at the desk, and slid the papers through the window in her direction.

"Here, I hope that's all you need." He'd barely sat back down when the woman called out to him again. She smiled and waved her fingers in the air for added effect.

"Mr. Frye? I'm sorry, but I need to see your driver's license."

Tom stood up, but didn't return to the desk. "What? Why do you need my driver's license?"

"We need to make a copy for your folder. You know," she smiled and paused, "just to make sure no one can impersonate you."

Tom stormed over to the receptionist and removed his license from his wallet. "You people are really something. Why would anyone want to impersonate someone at the doctor's office?" He threw his license on the desk and crossed his arms, waiting for a response.

"Oh, you'd be surprised," the young woman said, oblivious to Tom's sarcasm. "There are scammers everywhere. Even here." After photocopying it, she handed the license back and smiled. "Thanks. The nurse should come out to get you soon."

Tom stood there for a moment, staring at her.

By now the entire waiting room listened, anxious to hear what came next. To Vicky's probable relief, the nurse appeared simultaneously in the doorway, chart in hand.

"Tom Frye," she yelled in a loud voice.

After the perfunctory weight and blood pressure checks, Tom and Vicky sat in the office waiting for the doctor. Tom had lost weight since his last visit, but his blood pressure registered off the charts.

The chubby nurse made *tsk tsk* sounds. "Your blood pressure is high today. Dr. Martin will want to re-check it later in your exam."

Tom groaned and threw the nurse a dirty look. "You realize I'm probably dying here. You get that, right? I'm battling rabies."

"Tom. Stop. You're not 'battling' anything." Vicky addressed the nurse, "I'm sorry. He's a little upset."

"*Humph*," the nurse grunted. "The doctor will be in shortly." She scowled, assessing Tom once more before closing the door.

For twenty years, the entire Frye family had been patients of Dr. Jeff Martin, and he knew them well. Dr. Martin had a calm demeanor and a sly sense of humor. The whole family adored him.

"Tom, Vicky," Dr. Martin said walking into the exam room. "What brings you in today?" He went to a sink in the corner and washed up.

"I think I have rabies." Tom's eyes grew large, and he could feel his pulse racing. Sweat trickled down his face and neck.

Dr. Martin shared a puzzled look with Vicky. "Whoa, Tom. Slow down. What happened?" The doctor pulled up his wheeled padded stool and sat down at eye level with Tom.

"Well, I trimmed Christmas trees at the farm yesterday, and a black cat with a pink collar came close to where I was working and it bit me on my hand. I think I got too close to her kittens, and I—"

Dr. Martin held up a hand to stop Tom. "Oh, right. I forgot you bought Dennis' old nursery. How's that going?" The doctor looked unfazed.

"How's it going?" Tom ranted. "For God's sake, Doctor, I just told you a wild animal attacked me. I bent down to pet it and get a better look at her kittens, and she chomped down on me. I'm probably dying!" Tom waved his hand in front of the doctor. "Now it's infected. And I can't find the cat anywhere. Plus, then I saw this *other* black cat, too." Tom stopped talking when the doctor reached out and grabbed his forearm. Vicky looked shocked.

"Tom, calm down," Dr. Martin said. "Slow down. Black cats? Kittens? Petting stray animals?"

Now they were ganging up on him. "Yes, yes. I know. It was stupid. But the damn thing bit me and I don't know if it's had its rabies shots." Tom's face was bright red, and sweat matted his hair against his scalp.

"Let's have a look." Dr. Martin retrieved a small tray with antiseptic, cotton balls and some bandages. "Yep. Looks pretty nasty. On the road to infected, for sure." He cleaned the wound and then dotted a bandage with antiseptic ointment, wrapping the hand. "That should do it." The doctor stood and pushed the stool away with his foot.

"That's it? What a relief!" Tom practically jumped up and down.

"For the topical treatment, yes." Dr. Martin paused and put his hand on Tom's shoulder. "So, you never found the cat that bit you? Couldn't track it down?"

"No."

"I think we need to proceed with the vaccinations, then."

"The rabies shots? Seriously?"

"Yes, but it's not as bad as you think. They've improved over the years. It's very much like any other shot you might get. Flu shot, tetanus... Goes right in the arm, virtually painless."

"Wait," Tom stammered. "Not in the stomach? Multiple shots?"

"It's a series of shots, Tom. But they're in the arm. First, I'll give you a dose of immune globulin, and then four doses of rabies vaccines over a fourteen-day period. First dose today, then in three days you come back for another. Then back on days seven and fourteen."

"I guess there's no way to avoid it." Tom's shoulders slumped and Vicky stood and patted his back.

"Tom, the odds of this animal being rabid are pretty slim," Dr. Martin said, "but it's not worth taking any chances. If it had been a raccoon or bat, it'd be a no brainer to get the shots. We rarely hear about rabid cats in this part of the country." He scratched his chin in reflection. "It's not worth the stress. More of an inconvenience than anything else, coming back for the extra shots. But they're not bad."

The doctor sat at the computer and keyed in some information. "Listen, you two, I think while you're here, we'd better update your tetanus shots. You're both due. Might as well get it over with."

After the doctor left, the plump nurse returned with a tray of multiple injections. Tom looked down at her swollen feet popping out of the white nurse shoes, and wondered why anyone would torture their feet that way.

The nurse asked Tom to roll up his sleeve, and he took a few minutes to consider.

"Should I get the shot in my dominant arm? Or the other one?"

"What?" The nurse looked agitated.

"Which arm? Does it matter?"

"No."

"Okay, put it in my left arm then, I guess." Tom rolled up his sleeve and squeezed his eyes shut tight. He waited for the pinch, but after the cold cotton ball, he felt nothing, and kept waiting for what seemed like a long time. When he couldn't stand it anymore, he opened one eye to steal a peek, in perfect time to see the nasty nurse, headed toward him with the massive needle. Everything went black.

When he came to, he was lying down on the exam table with a pillow under his head and a cool compress over his eyes. He removed the washcloth and saw Vicky standing over him frowning.

"He's awake. Nurse!" Vicky sounded irritated.

The plump woman walked over to the exam table and peered into Tom's eyes with her little flashlight. "Okay, his pupils look normal. Time to sit up, sweet pea."

She grabbed Tom's forearm and pulled him to a sitting position.

"How're you feeling? Better? You're all done for today." The nurse smirked and added, "This is the first time I've ever seen a grown man pass out getting a shot. And I've been a nurse for twenty years. This'll give me a story to tell my husband tonight."

"Thanks," Tom said. "Glad to help."

"Ha, ha, ha! You're a funny one."

"Yeah, I've heard that before."

"You're all set to go," the nurse said. "Hold on while I get the wheelchair for you. Oh, and here's your paperwork for the front desk. They'll schedule your next appointment. Hang on one sec..."

"I don't need a wheelchair. I'm fine now."

"Sorry, sweet pea." The nurse smirked again. "Standard procedure—you faint, you get a wheelchair. No driving."

Tom yelled out as the nurse guided him into the wheelchair. "Vick?"

"I'm right here, honey. I'll meet you at the desk."

Vicky scheduled Tom's appointments while he sat embarrassed in the wheelchair. The snarky nurse cracked her gum and tapped her plump foot to the beat of the elevator music playing in the waiting room. With multiple appointments scheduled, Tom, Vicky and the nurse wheeled through the automatic doors and looked for their car.

"Yoo hoo!" called a familiar voice from across the parking lot. "Tom! Vicky! Hello."

Keeping his head down, Tom caught a glimpse of beige polyester legs moving in his direction. *Oh God, I can't see my old secretary now.*

"Oh hi, Peggy," said Vicky. "How're you doing?"

"I'm good," Peggy answered. Her hair looked unwashed. She pulled her tight tee shirt down to cover her stomach. "Here to pick up refills for my husband's meds. Better than you guys, I guess. What happened, Tom?" She bent down to try to make eye contact with her former boss.

"I was attacked. By a wild animal," Tom raved. "I needed to get treatment."

"Oh! That's awful," said Peggy. "Was it another bird?"

"Cat," Vicky chuckled. "Tom found a mother cat and her litter of kittens and couldn't resist disturbing them. The mother cat bit him. We couldn't track her down to find the owner. So..." Vicky waved her arm and gestured to Tom in the wheelchair.

Peggy appeared to stifle a giggle. "Huh, cat. Well, that's funny."

"There's nothing funny about rabies shots, Peggy." Tom felt his blood pressure boiling. "What's wrong with you?"

"Well, of course it's not *funny*, but you know... ironic." Peggy smiled. "I mean, Tom, you, of all people, petting a strange cat. I remember how you always complained about your girls' cats, how much you didn't like them."

"Yes, Peggy. I'm aware."

"Are we done chit-chatting here, people? I've got to get back to work," the chubby nurse barked. "Slide your behind out of this chair and into your car, Mr. Frye."

Tom air-slapped at the nurse when she attempted to help him out of the wheelchair. "I am perfectly capable of getting into my own car, thank you. You're dismissed." He climbed into the passenger seat and rolled down the window.

"Ha. That's funny." The nurse laughed. "*Dismissed.* You're a real piece of work, aren't you?"

Tom glared as the woman pushed the wheelchair toward the medical center, still chuckling to herself. A few steps later she turned and waved, calling out, "See you in three days."

"I'm sorry, Tom. Truly," Peggy said. "But hey, how's everything at the store?"

"Things are good," Vicky piped up, starting the engine. "We're crazy busy. And most of our seasonal help will be headed back to school soon. I dread looking for people to hire."

"What's happening at Global Financial these days, Peggy?" Tom couldn't resist asking.

"Why, do you miss it? You should come and visit once in a while." Peggy smiled and blew a bubble with her gum. Tom's face grew red with embarrassment. "What's wrong, Tom? Afraid you'll want to come back? You know, lots of your old clients ask about you all of the time."

"Well, that's nice to hear," Tom said straightening up in his seat. "But I'm pretty busy. Got my hands full, you know?"

"Is that right?" Peggy asked. "Too bad. I know they'd love to have you come back." She blew another bubble and cracked the gum. "Of course, Lance is the same as ever. So..."

Vicky smiled through gritted teeth and gave Peggy the thumbs up signal. She dropped the car into gear. "Great to see you, Peggy. Take care."

Peggy moved closer and leaned into the window. "Yeah, you guys too. I better get this script filled. My husband's not good." She lowered her voice to a whisper. "He's been having some issues. Anxiety." Shrugging her shoulders, she held up the empty pill bottle and started walking toward the medical center, waving goodbye.

For the first time in a couple of days, Tom felt better. Peggy's comments cheered him. It was nice to hear that clients kept asking about him, even after several years out of the business. He missed some of them... and others, not at all. He couldn't help but wonder. *Did I leave too soon?*

CHAPTER 3

The next morning, the Fryes drove to work in silence. Vicky glanced at Tom out of the corner of her eye from time to time.

"You're quiet. Everything okay?"

"Yeah, I'm sorry, Vick. It's Peggy's fault. She has me second-guessing myself."

"Oh please, Tom. What a bunch of bull." Vicky slowed the car as she pulled into the Country Bumpkin's parking lot. "You can't seriously be having doubts now? After five years?" She got out of the car, slamming the door.

"Vick, wait. Please," Tom called from inside the car to his wife, but she walked ahead through the sliding glass doors and into the nursery. He realized how ridiculous that sounded to her. But he couldn't help it.

After waiting a few more minutes, he got out of the car and walked across the parking lot. He ran into Walter watering the trees marked for end of the summer clearance. He called to him and ventured over.

Walter, tall and lanky looked like he hadn't aged a bit in all the years Tom had known him. He waved to his boss and dropped the hose, preparing to shake hands. But Tom declined and held up his bandaged right hand in explanation.

"Oh hey, what happened to you, boss?"

"It's a long story, Walter." Tom kicked a few stones around on the ground before he answered. "I got attacked. By some crazy-ass black cat protecting her kittens."

"A black cat? It wasn't Kitty, was it?"

"Did you say Kitty? Big black cat, pink collar?"

"Yeah, that's her. That's Mrs. Simpson's cat. You know the lady that lives in the little brick house on the corner, across from our storage shed? She's one of Vicky's rose customers."

For a moment Tom thought he might pass out. His hands started shaking. "Jesus, Walter, I had to get a rabies vaccination! And I have three more shots to go." *I knew it, a neighborhood cat. All those shots for nothing?* He tried to steady himself. "Do you think that old lady takes her cat to the vet?"

Walter paused and looked at Tom's hand before he spoke again. "Hmmm, don't know. Hard to say. But I know she dotes on that cat. I remember the day she got her."

"Really?" Tom raised an eyebrow.

"Yeah, odd the way that happened. Mrs. Stab showed up one day with a basket of kittens. One of her cats just had another litter and she wanted to know if we wanted any to keep around the store."

Tom interrupted. "Wait a minute! What did you say about a Mrs. Stab? As in Mina Stab?"

"Yep. That's the one." Walter nodded in agreement. "She lives up over the hill, remember? She thought maybe we might like to have a couple cats around. You know, to keep out the mice, voles, those kinds of critters. You remember, she was a big customer when Dennis was still alive?"

Tom winced. "Yes. I'm aware." *Walter must not realize the history Mina and I share.*

"Yeah, so Mrs. Simpson was here that day and Mina talked her into taking one of the kittens. Another lady took one, too. I don't remember much about her." Walter stopped to take a drink from his water bottle. "But how'd you get bitten? I didn't think Kitty wandered so far from home."

"I was trimming Christmas trees on the hill when I saw her with the litter. I got too close, and she chomped down pretty hard. I left to get the bite cleaned off, and by the time I got back to where I last saw her, the damned cat had moved the kittens. I haven't seen her since."

"Tough break, man," Walter said with a smirk. "Well, Mrs. Simpson lives right over there," he said pointing toward the horizon. "Why don't you ask her?"

"Thanks, I think I will. But first I've got some stuff to take care of inside the store."

Tom intended to go straight to his office and dive into the books, but he found himself distracted by the TV in the reception area. The HGTV station blared all day, regardless of whether anyone watched or not.

"So this is why the electric bill is eight hundred dollars this month," he said aloud. His bandaged hand reached up to grab the remote, but he paused. *I wonder how the market is doing today.* He peeked around the corner and spotted Vicky in her office with the assistant manager, Heather... or Hyacinth or some kind of plant name... hovering over what he assumed was the schedule for next month.

Instead of clicking the TV off, he switched the channel to MSNBC. Immediately a rush came over him. His pulse quickened as his eyes drifted to the bottom of the screen. *Oh, the DOW's up 158 points. Nice.* He stood mesmerized and didn't notice Vicky walking toward him.

"Tom?" Her tone sounded accusatory. A frown creased her forehead.

"Hey." He clicked the TV off and returned the remote to its designated spot.

"What're you doing? Why are you watching that?"

Tom cleared his throat and struggled for an explanation. "Well, I came over to turn the TV off. Nobody was watching. Then I wondered how the markets were doing today."

"Really? You know the psychiatrist said you should distance yourself from that stuff. I don't like it."

"Vick, listen. I may not be managing other people's money anymore, but I have to keep an eye on our investments, don't I? You do realize we have accounts that are affected by the fluctuation of the markets? Just like everybody else?" He paused for effect. "Hello? Understood?"

"I don't believe you." Vicky put hands on hips and sharpened her gaze.

"Honest, honey. I'm fine. As a matter of fact, I'm headed straight back to my office to pay the bills from last month." He raised his wrapped hand in oath-taking position. "I swear."

He started walking away then stopped and turned around. "Oh, I found out who owns the cat that bit me. Mrs. Simpson. From down the road?"

"Really? The Mrs. Simpson who buys so many rose bushes?"

"That's her. I'm gonna head over there later this afternoon and see if Kitty was kept up to date with her vaccinations."

"Yeah, good. Maybe you won't need the rest of those shots."

"Here's hoping. See you later."

After paying the bills, Tom walked across the field in the direction of elderly Mrs. Simpson's house and he started to feel better. He hoped to God he wouldn't need to have any more shots.

When Mrs. Simpson answered her front door, no sign of recognition crossed her face. "Yes?"

"Hi, I'm Tom Frye. I own The Country Bumpkin nursery?"

"Oh, hello! I'm sorry I didn't recognize you without my glasses. I was getting ready to take a bath when I heard the doorbell."

"Well, I beg your pardon, ma'am. I don't mean to disturb you, but do you have a few minutes to chat? I have a couple of questions about your cat."

"My cat?" Mrs. Simpson kept the door partially closed and didn't invite Tom inside.

"Yes, ma'am. You see she had her kittens under one of our pine trees on the Christmas tree farm, and when I got too close, she bit me." He held up his bandaged hand as evidence. Mrs. Simpson looked surprised. Tom continued, "Well, frankly, I didn't know who owned the cat. I assumed she had an owner because I saw her nametag, but when I searched for her later, I couldn't find her anywhere."

Mrs. Simpson stared at Tom, not saying a word.

"I had to have shots—rabies shots—because I couldn't locate the cat. My employee, Walter was out on vacation last week, and it wasn't until he came home that I learned it was your cat. You know Walter? Right? Big, tall guy…"

"My cat is very sweet, Mr. Frye. I don't think she'd bite anyone."

"Yes, ma'am. I'm sure she's very sweet. To you, I mean, but she bit me. Hard. Like a puncture wound? It looked infected right away, so my doctor thought we needed to take precautions. Just in case."

"In case of what, Mr. Frye?"

"If she hadn't had her rabies shots."

"Well, I'm sure she has. Let me think… hmmm. When did I take Kitty to the vet last?" Mrs. Simpson smiled. "She hates going to the vet, my little Kitty. Just despises getting in the car." She chuckled.

"Yes, ma'am. I'm sure she does. I know all about cats and cars. Have two myself. But I need to make sure she's been vaccinated. Or else I'm gonna have to finish getting the other rounds of rabies shots. And I'd rather not."

"Certainly," Mrs. Simpson said, nodding her curly gray head.

"Do you have the tags from the vet? Those little tags they give you when you've gotten the shots?"

"Well, I suppose I might have them somewhere. I don't know. But right now I'm going to take my bath and get ready to watch my shows."

"Uh-huh, okay." Tom's patience evaporated more by the second. "Do you think you could check, real quick and see if you can find them? Since I'm here and everything?"

"Mr. Frye, as I told you, I'm about to take a bath. This is not a good time for me."

"Yes ma'am, and I apologize for that, but you must have a place where you keep important papers and things? A place you could quickly check for the tags? Before your bath?"

"No. I don't think so, Mr. Frye. Not today. I'll look for them another day. Maybe tomorrow. Or the day after. Goodbye." Mrs. Simpson moved to close the door, but Tom pushed against it with his good hand.

"Mrs. Simpson, I'm begging you, please. Can you look now?"

"No, I won't." The feisty older woman pushed back to close it, but Tom was much stronger.

"Please! Jesus Christ! What's wrong with you? *Your* animal attacked me! Unprovoked on *my* property. Do I need to go to the authorities to get you to cooperate?"

"Young man. I don't like your tone, and I don't approve of cursing. Get off my property now, or I'll call the police myself!" She pushed harder against the door.

Well, I pissed off the old bat now. Think. How can I fix this?

Tom cleared his throat and lowered his voice. "Mrs. Simpson, I'm sure it's important for you to watch your television show, Lawrence Welk or whomever, but this is serious." He stooped lower to attempt eye contact with the old lady, but she looked angrier than ever. "Please. Could you look for the tags?"

"I told you no, Mr. Frye. Now get off my property." She slammed the door.

Tom smacked himself in the head, making his sore hand throb again. In frustration, he backed off the doorstep and started down her driveway. But he stopped midway, grabbed the baseball cap off his head, then screamed into it.

Mrs. Simpson opened the door again and called after him. "And by the way, I'm watching *Sex in the City*. So there!"

Furious, Tom stormed off. No doubt his blood pressure skyrocketed. Good thing he'd decided to walk over here. He needed to blow off some steam. The nerve of that old crone, refusing to look for the rabies tags. Who wouldn't at least pretend to look around for the damn things? As soon as he got home, he needed to call his attorney buddy, Jim Doyle, and get his take on this crazy situation.

All the way back to the Country Bumpkin, Tom fumed thinking about Mrs. Simpson's refusal to help. The parking lot had cleared out, no sign of Vicky's car anywhere. Time to close up shop for the night. God, he needed a beer and a good hot shower. He double-checked all the doors had been locked and that Vicky had set the alarm. Then, he heard the bleep of a siren and turned to see a cop car pulling into the parking lot. With gravel flying, it stopped in front of Tom.

"Mr. Frye?" asked the cop. "We need to ask you a few questions."

CHAPTER 4

Tom expected the cops to sympathize with the story he recanted, but the young police officer kept a stony face while taking down Tom's side of the story.

"So, you started cursing at her after she refused to look for the rabies tags? Correct?" the cop questioned.

"Y-y-yes," Tom stammered. "I mean, no. I didn't curse at her exactly."

"According to Mrs. Simpson, you insulted her." The cop looked down at his notepad. "Something about watching Lawrence Welk?" The cop cleared his throat.

Tom's eyebrows knitted together in a scowl. "Yeah. I mean, I guess so. But I didn't mean to insult her. I just assumed..."

The cop said nothing and looked annoyed.

Tom tried to smile and shrugged his shoulders. *Cops look way too young these days.* He craned his neck to read the nametag on the guy's uniform. *Maybe he's not really a policeman. Nah. How else would he know about what happened?*

"Well now, Mr. Frye, I don't anticipate you heading back over there and bothering Mrs. Simpson again, so I'll leave you with a warning. However, if I were you..." At this point the young officer pulled off his mirrored aviator sunglasses and looked into Tom's eyes. "...I'd keep off Mrs. Simpson's property." The cop chuckled a bit. "She's prepared to charge you with the attempted kidnapping of her cat, harassment, trespassing and whatever else she can conjure up. Watch yourself."

Tom's foot found a large pebble in the gravel parking lot and gave it a swift kick toward the building. "Yeah. Okay. I get it." He raked his hand through his hair. "But I'm the victim here. I'm innocent. Her animal attacked me on *my* property. Now I have to finish getting rabies shots and—"

The officer held up his hand, interrupting Tom's rant. "Irrelevant to me, sir. It's all hearsay. Now if you'll just sign on the dotted line, acknowledging that you've officially been warned, I'll be on my way." He thrust a clipboard, pen and a form with print too tiny for any human to read in Tom's direction. Tom moved the clipboard up and down to try to focus, but it was useless.

Dammit, I can't see a thing. He fished his reading glasses out of his shirt pocket and scanned the document. *This is such a bunch of bullshit.* Frustrated, Tom scribbled his name and dated the form before handing it back to the policeman. Now that he had his glasses, he saw the cop's name clearly: Officer Friendly. "I have to say, I think all this is unfair. Other than that, I'm speechless," he muttered.

"Not a bad thing," said the officer. "You have a good day, sir."

"Yeah, thanks." He watched the policeman open the car door. "Hey, is that really your name? Officer Friendly? That's pretty funny."

Again, the cop removed his sunglasses and stared at Tom. He reached down and tapped his nametag twice. "Yes. It's my real name." Then his hand moved to his gun holster and lingered there a few moments. His fingers drummed the leather. "Any other questions?"

"Nope." Tom seethed watching Officer Friendly peel out onto the main road. "Fucker," he said as the cop drove into the distance.

***

Doyle didn't answer his cell, and when Tom tried the landline the ringing went on forever. Disgusted, he left a second message and chugged his third Heineken.

"Doyle. You bastard. Call me back. It's important. Later."

The sound of the garage door alerted Tom to Vicky's return. He glanced at his watch—nine-thirty, kind of late for a Monday night.

"Hello?" Vicky's voice echoed through the kitchen into the family room where Tom sprawled on the couch. The television blared *Bar Rescue*, his new favorite show.

"Hey Vick, how was the Chamber gig?"

Vicky walked over to tousle Tom's hair and bent down to give him a kiss on the cheek. "Good. Fun. Lots of people showed up. I saw Doyle there." Vicky kicked off her sandals and propped up her feet on the coffee table. "He never changes, does he?"

"Ha! Nope. Why, was he hitting on some poor woman?" Tom snickered at the thought.

"Of course. He latched onto some college intern who works for the Chamber. She was in charge of selling raffle tickets, and he hung around her booth all night. At least he harassed people to stop and buy tickets, so I guess he did her a favor."

"Yeah, sounds like him. Did you buy any?"

"Of course. You know how lucky I am." Vicky rubbed her hands together. "I bought a roll of tickets for thirty bucks. They had some pretty cool prizes donated this year. Who knows, maybe I'll win something exciting."

"I'm sure you will, babe." Tom got up and walked to the refrigerator. "Hey, do you want a glass of wine? I'm having a beer."

"You mean you're having *another* beer? Sure, why not? I'll join you."

Tom scowled as he poured her rosé. She sniffed out his drinking every time. He had barely sat down when his cell vibrated in his pocket. No doubt Doyle was returning his call.

"Doyle," Tom said into the phone as he put it on speaker.

"FUCKING FRYE MAN! YOU ASSHOLE! WHAT'S YOUR PROBLEM?"

"What do you mean, what's my problem? And there happens to be a lady present, so watch your mouth, you piece of shit."

Doyle began to guffaw. "Ah, the Lady Victoria is home already? She looked FINE this evening, my friend, and lots of dudes checked out your hot wife, too. How come you didn't come along?"

"Eh, it's a long story, man."

"HAHAHA! Vicky told me about your little rabies scare. Classy, dude, very classy."

"What? Seriously? You're giving me shit about this, too? Listen man, I almost got arrested tonight because of those rabies shots."

"Excuse me?" Vicky chimed in. "Arrested?"

"Hello, sexy lady," Doyle blurted out. "Hey, Vick? Do me a solid and get me that little chippie from the Chamber's phone number?"

"Hi again, Jim," Vicky said. "No way. That girl refused you for a reason."

"Traitor. Okay. Put Fryeman back on." Doyle chuckled.

Vicky got up from the couch and took her glass of wine out into the kitchen. "I'll eavesdrop from out here while you explain your legal problems."

Doyle hooted with laughter as Tom explained the black cat sightings, the series of rabies shots, his encounter with Mrs. Simpson, and the subsequent arrival of Officer Friendly.

"Only you, brother. This could only happen to you." Doyle continued to laugh.

"Doyle, this isn't funny, you asshole. This old lady is bat-shit crazy. What if she comes after me? Plus, now I have to finish getting those stupid shots."

"As usual, you are blowing this WAY out of proportion, Fryeman. Settle down. The old lady's not gonna go after you...

although you might've lost a good customer. Vicky said she buys a lot of roses from you guys."

"Yeah, she used to anyway. But it's the principle of the thing, Doyle. *Her* animal attacked me on *my* property. Shouldn't that account for something?" Tom's voice escalated as he pounded his fist on the coffee table, causing him to howl in pain again. Vicky rose from her barstool at the kitchen island and glared.

"In a word, no," said Doyle. "Man, a jury is never gonna go against a mother cat with kittens owned by some rose-loving widow. And I'd bet my last dollar a judge wouldn't either. You're screwed. Give it up."

"Well, fuck you, too," Tom screamed into his phone. He hung up and whipped the cell against the couch cushions.

Vicky strolled into the family room and plopped down beside him. "So Mrs. Simpson wouldn't help you? What happened? She called the police?"

"The old bat said I interrupted her bath and TV time. It didn't suit her to look for the tags today."

"Huh. I'm surprised." Vicky took a sip of her wine and swirled it around in the glass. "She's always very sweet when she stops in at the nursery."

"Well, she wasn't sweet today, I can assure you. She's insane, I think."

"Tom, you think everyone is 'insane'. And besides, I'm sure she'll change her mind and look for the tags."

"I don't think so, Vick." Tom guzzled a big swallow of his beer and released a monstrous belch. "She was very pissed off. I kind of lost my temper. I may have cursed."

"What? Oh Tom, you didn't? That's beneath you. I remember you always had a soft spot for widows when you were a broker." Vicky tried to meet Tom's gaze, but he averted his eyes. "Did the police really show up at the nursery?"

"Unfortunately, yeah. But it's fine. I told the cop my side of the story and he left."

"Hmmm. Well, she's not coming back to buy any more roses from us if you cursed at her."

"Yeah, well good riddance! I didn't like her one bit. We don't need customers like her anyway." Tom finished his beer and started to walk into the kitchen for another when the doorbell interrupted him. "What the hell?" He put his empty bottle on the counter and walked to the door. "Jesus, it's 10:15."

"Maybe it's one of the kids' friends. See who's there."

Tom opened the door and found himself staring at the tall, muscular frame of Officer Friendly.

"Officer?" Tom attempted to keep his voice steady. "Two visits in one day?"

"Thomas Frye?"

Tom rolled his eyes. "Yes. You know it's me. We met earlier. At my nursery."

Officer Friendly thrust an official looking document at Tom and gestured for him to accept it. "Mr. Frye, consider yourself served. Mrs. Helena Simpson has filed a PFA against you, sir."

"What? What in God's name are you talking about? A PFA? What's that all about?"

"Protection From Abuse, sir," the young cop said.

"Yes, I know what a PFA is," Tom shouted. "I'm not a fucking idiot, you know."

"Tom!" Vicky rose and walked to the front door.

"Mr. Frye, I believe I've already cautioned you about your language once this evening. Don't make me write you up for public drunkenness and disorderly conduct."

"Public drunkenness? Don't be ridiculous. I'm in my own home. I can conduct myself however I please."

Vicky pushed Tom to the side. "Tom. Stop. Officer, we want to cooperate, of course. Please, can you tell me what this is all about?"

"Ma'am, Mrs. Simpson has filed a PFA against your husband. She claims she's afraid he'll be back to harass her."

"That's ridiculous!" Tom screamed. "I'm the wronged party here. I'm the one who has to keep getting these damned rabies shots. She refused to help me! Wouldn't even look for the rabies tags for her cat." Tom's eyes looked wild. "How did she manage to get a PFA so quickly?"

The cop pulled the document out of Tom's hands and pointed at the bottom of the page. "Here you go. Signed by the Honorable Randall P. Simpson, Magistrate of the Fourth District of the Commonwealth of Pennsylvania. Mrs. Simpson's son."

Tom, no stranger to the power of nepotism, nodded in understanding.

"If you don't have any other questions, I'll be on my way. But if I were you, I'd get a lawyer."

"Gee, thanks a million," Tom said and slammed the front door. He picked up his phone and called Doyle back.

CHAPTER 5

D oyle refused to answer Tom's call that night. On the phone the next morning, he explained, "I was busy. You know. With the neighbor lady across the street."

"Busy? Jesus, Doyle. You're such a player."

"What can I say, brother? I have uncontrollable animal magnetism."

"Screw you and your magnetism. Did you listen to my message?"

Doyle howled with laughter on the other end of the phone. "Yeah, tough break, dude. Only you would pick a fight with the District Magistrate's mother."

Tom pulled the phone away from his ear and gritted his teeth. His best friend relished seeing him tortured.

"Enough about that, Doyle. Do I have any recourse here?"

"Nah, I mean not recourse timely enough to help you. By the time we counter-file something against her, you'd have to complete the shots anyway. My advice is to avoid the old lady and move on."

Tom blew out an angry breath. "Fine." He hung up on Doyle. Enough wasted time worrying about Mrs. Simpson. Today he needed to round up all the plants to discount for the fall sale. But by the time he walked to the Reduced for Quick Sale section of the nursery, Walter had a good start on sorting the saleable trees and shrubs.

"Morning, Tom," Walter called as he waved to his boss. "I've got most of these trees tagged for reduction and I'm ready to start on the shrubs and perennials."

"Good. Thanks, Walter. Anything else going on here I should know about?"

"Nah, it's been pretty quiet. So far, so good." Walter paused and took a sip from his thermos. "Always sad to see the end of summer. Even with all the hard work we do, it sure beats the hell out of shoveling snow and selling Christmas trees."

Tom snorted. "Jesus, don't remind me. I need to get up to the tree farm and finish trimming. Plus, I've got a million things to take care of before we send Sophie back to college. Before I know it, they'll both be college graduates, getting married. Then we'll be true empty nesters. It's hard to believe."

"Yep. They grow up fast. My boy's gonna be graduating next year. Hope that baseball scholarship comes through. Otherwise, my savings account is toast."

Together they sorted through the shrubs and perennials. The annual plants were a total write-off, along with anything else they couldn't sell. In a few hours' time they had set up an attractive display near the front entrance of the nursery.

"Hey Walt, I'm headed inside to find Vicky. I'm pretty sure I need to get the rest of my shots today."

"Oh, yeah. I forgot about the shots," said Walter. "How'd you make out with Mrs. Simpson? She help you out?"

"Don't get me started. What a freaking nightmare that was." Tom shook his head. "No. Let's say I've made a new enemy. She refused to look for the rabies tags. Called the cops on me. Had me served with a PFA. Unbelievable."

"What? You're shitting me?"

"Nope. Long story. I'll tell you about it someday. But I think it's safe to say we've lost Mrs. Simpson as a customer. Talk to you later, man."

"Okay, boss. Catch you later."

Inside the store, Tom found Vicky looking over the books. He patted the top of her head in greeting.

"Hey, hon. Did you manage to talk to Doyle?"

"Ha! That asshole. Yes. No help. As usual."

"Tom, watch your language in the store. You're going to alienate all of our customers if you keep swearing like a drunken sailor."

"Bullshit!" Tom said, raising his voice. "I don't give a damn. I wish I *were* drunk. I'm sick of this whole thing."

"Thomas, stop right now before someone hears you. Don't act so childish. You're fifty-five years old. You can't keep changing jobs every few years."

"Yeah, yeah, I hear you. I'm outta here. I need to finish trimming up the Christmas trees."

"Well, for God's sake, don't pet any stray animals."

"Ha, ha. So funny, Vick. You're quite the comedienne." He stormed off and grabbed his ladder and tools from the shed and hiked up the hill.

The sultry, late summer heat radiated off the aluminum ladder. Tom calmed down once he got to work. With his earbuds in place blaring classic rock, and the shears in hand, his anxiety evaporated. It reminded him of why he'd left the financial world. Here he felt peace and had a clear mission. Shaping the evergreens into their classic pyramidal form, he could picture how they'd look in a few months, propped up for sale with twinkling lights under frosty December skies.

After he trimmed a number of pines, he prepared to drag his ladder to the next row of trees. A rustling noise caught his attention. He stopped and waited, wondering if there might be a snake in the grass. Then he heard it, the distinct meowing, coming from behind a large pine tree.

Oh no, not again. Please God, no.

And then he saw it. The pink collar, the sleek black fur, back arched in a languid stretch. Kitty!

"Son of a bitch!" he yelled out loud. "Jesus. Not this cat again."

Kitty, oblivious to the distress she caused Tom, lifted a back paw and scratched behind her ears. She continued to scratch and groom herself, causing the tiny silver bell on her collar to tinkle. Tom remained immobile, unsure what to do.

Jesus H. Christ, I think I'm afraid of this cat. Or her owner. Or both.

Tom took a tentative step forward, dragging the ladder along with him. The cat startled and began to hiss, raising her paw in defense.

"Whoa there, cat. Keep your distance. Back! Back!" Tom threw down his pruning shears and used the ladder to block the animal, much like a lion tamer in the circus.

The cat hissed again, swatted its paw one final time and took off across the field toward Mrs. Simpson's property.

Tom's beating heart thumped and a fresh stream of sweat poured down his face. He put up the ladder and used it for support. He took a swig from his water jug and tried to regain calm. Once his breathing slowed, he walked around the trees to see if the kittens were anywhere nearby. But no sign of the tiny creatures could be found anywhere.

Good. Thank God for that, at least. She must've moved them again. I guess that damned cat is going to continue to torture me. I need to ignore it, and not let it upset me. Even though it makes me mad all over again. Stupid Mrs. Simpson.

"Argghh!" He let the anger out with a single, caveman rant, forcing himself to let it go. He took a deep breath, took another sip of water and decided to shake it off and get back to work. *How did this happen? Be careful what you wish for,* he thought. *Here I am, busting my balls, sweating like a pig and fighting off stray cats. God, I wish I could transport myself back in time to my old office, with my feet propped up watching MSNBC.*

He resumed a decent rhythm of pruning, cleaning up the clippings and moving down the line of pine trees. Soon he'd have to wrap up and head over to the doctor's office for his last round of shots. Every time he thought about it, rage swept over him anew.

This is not fair! I shouldn't have to get the rest of these shots if that cat had all the proper vaccinations.

"Well, since I've managed to get myself all worked up again, I might as well call it a day," he said to no one in particular. That's when it appeared again between the rows of evergreens, racing down the path headed right for him. It moved like a panther in the jungle hunting its prey. The cat came within a foot of Tom and stopped in its tracks. In the stillness of the pine trees its meow roared in his ears.

"Ah ha! It's you. Back for another bite, Kitty?" Tom taunted. The cat, silent now, stared into Tom's eyes. He shivered.

Maybe this cat is possessed? Like, some demon cat from Hell here to torment me. Nah, that can't be possible. Can it? Maybe it wasn't a cat, but the ghost of some old dissatisfied client who passed away, come back from the dead to drive me crazy.

Something in his mind churned as he and the cat continued their staring contest. Should he try to pick up the cat again? See if the rabies tags were on its collar? Yes, that might work. His family cats had their rabies tags on their collars, along with their identification tags. He couldn't miss this opportunity.

Very slowly he pulled his work gloves from his back pockets and put them on, moving as little as possible. He waited for what felt like an eternity and took a small step forward. Step by step he crept closer until the cat was within grabbing distance. Locked into their staring contest, Kitty and Tom never lost eye contact. When he could reach the cat, he scooped her up into his arms and held her tight, looking for the tags. And then, he had it in his fingers—Kitty's ID tag and the steely gray rabies tag, complete with the information he'd hoped for. Kitty had received her two-year rabies vaccination.

After double-checking the dates, he tossed her to the soft pine needles under the nearest tree. With a final glance back to her nemesis and a loud hiss, Kitty took off running. Smiling ear to ear, Tom gathered up his tools and laughed all the way back to the nursery.

CHAPTER 6

With the drama of the rabies shots and PFA behind him, Tom looked forward to life returning to normal, and prepared to send Sophie off for her junior year of college in Philadelphia. Two hours away, Temple offered the Theatre Arts major she wanted, as well as the chance to live independently.

He took some time to run on the treadmill then grabbed a late breakfast and another coffee.

"Sophie, how's the packing coming?"

"Uh yeah, about that. I need help," Sophie sputtered.

"Let's not overstate the obvious," Vicky called from the laundry room.

"Mo-ther. *Stop.* You're not helping."

"Soph, did you even get started yet? You're leaving in three days." Tom's volume increased.

"Well, mentally, yes. I know what I need to pack. I haven't done any actual packing yet, though."

"Jesus H., girl. What have you been doing? You stopped working at the nursery two weeks ago to 'start packing for school.' Are you telling me you haven't started at all?"

"That's what's I'm saying. Yes." Sophie returned her attention to the cell in her hand.

"I hope you're not expecting Mommy to do all the work for you."

"No, of course not. I'm starting today, after I take a nap."

"It's 11:00. You got up at 9:30. How can you need a nap?"

"I'm tired, Daddy. I didn't sleep well. I'm worried about my new roommates. I've never met two of them. And four people in one apartment. That's a lot of people."

"So why didn't you get up and start packing if you're so worried? Put down your damn phone and get to work. *Now!*"

Sophie rolled her eyes and looked to her mother for help. Vicky smirked and kept folding clothes. "Good idea. I'll be up to help after I finish the laundry."

Tom shook his head. "Wait, let me ask the obvious question. Does she have any boxes?"

"Only because I went to Costco and scarfed some from the free box bin."

"Vicky, how in the hell are they ever going to learn to be independent if you keep coming to the rescue? The helicopter needs to land and return to the heliport."

"Very funny, mister. How do you think anything gets done around here without my helicopter parenting? I am on their backs twenty-four/seven. It's not fun. I'm exhausted."

"So stop."

"And do what, Tom? Cross my arms like Jeannie and blink, waiting for boxes to appear on their own? Wiggle my nose like Samantha from *Bewitched* and imagine a fully loaded U-Haul complete with a handsome driver?" Vicky dropped the laundry basket on the floor and threw in the rest of the unfolded clothes from the dryer. "Honestly, you're as bad as they are. I'm so tired of nagging people all the time. If it's not here at home, I'm lighting a fire under those part-time kids we hired to help at the nursery."

Tom frowned and opened the refrigerator for a beer. When he saw Vicky's expression, he changed his mind, and grabbed the jug of grapefruit juice instead. He opened it up and slurped a few gulps before putting it back in the fridge.

"Nice. Real classy, Tom. There's no need to wonder where the girls get their manners."

Loud stomping up and down the steps to retrieve boxes interrupted the silence between Tom and Vicky. Clearly Sophie preferred to work on something else. They heard her dropping suitcases and boxes on the floor, putting her years of theatrical training to use. Despite their frustration, they chuckled. Sophie had a reputation as a terrible procrastinator.

Tom walked over and grabbed Vicky in a bear hug. "I'm sorry, babe, you know we'd be lost without you."

Placated, Vicky returned his embrace and returned to folding the laundry.

"Well, since she's started packing, I'm going over to the nursery," Tom said. "I've got a bunch of stuff to finish up before we take her back to school this weekend."

"Okay. Goodbye. You can leave now. I'm going to help our daughter pack." Vicky waved and jogged up the steps.

When he got to the store, he balanced the books, checked over the inventory and blared the television in his office. With Vicky out of the store for a few days, he watched MSNBC openly and relished his defiance. Since he'd be gone both Saturday and Sunday, he reminded Walter what needed to be taken care of over the weekend.

"Mrs. Stab came in here this morning, boss," Walter said. "She wants us to give her a quote for some landscaping ideas."

"What? Mina? No! I thought she vowed never to do business with the Bumpkin after Dennis died on her farm."

"Yeah, I got the feeling she's had trouble finding good help. Made it sound like you and her were old pals, and she wanted to work with us again."

"Ha! That's a laugh. That woman drove me crazy." Tom paused and scratched his chin. "But sales are down for the landscaping services, and frankly, we could use the revenue."

"Amen to that, chief. I told her I'd drive over this weekend and have a look. Try to figure out what she needs, give her some ideas." Walter smiled. "That is, if you're okay with it?"

"Ah, what the hell. Why not? Revenge is a dish best served cold." Tom grinned. "Might as well bring in some old financial clients as new landscaping customers." Tom packed up his paperwork and grabbed his keys. "Hey, I'll see you, man. I'm out of here."

"Adios, Tom. And good luck getting the kiddo off to Temple."

"Yeah, thanks. Sophie's a mess. Vicky's at home doing all the packing for her. Not sure how that girl will survive on her own."

"Eh, she'll find her way. Most of them figure it out."

"I guess. Well okay, see you on Monday." Tom walked out the door, but changed his mind, pulling a U-turn in the parking lot and hurrying back inside the store. At his desk, he turned on the computer and scanned the closed customer accounts, looking for the Stab's prior landscaping services. The numbers looked impressive, but it might be a tough pill to swallow, having them as customers. After reviewing the information again, he printed it to take along.

Tom decided to take the long way home, and swing by the Stab estate to get a sneak peek before Walter got there that weekend. The drive along the back roads relaxed him and allowed plenty of time to workshop some costly landscape upgrades for those miserable people. Right off the top of his head, he thought of a bunch of great ideas, like a pond or fancy fountain that would cost them a small fortune. The more he thought about it, the more excited he got. Mina's interest presented an excellent opportunity. Providence had given him the chance to put the screws to the Stabs for a change, instead of vice versa.

CHAPTER 7

As predicted, Sophie's trademark procrastination stressed the entire family. Even Jane lent a hand, carrying boxes from her sister's bedroom to load into the family SUV.

"Jane, it's very nice of you to help, sweetie," Vicky said.

"Well, for God's sake, Mom. I couldn't stand to listen to her crying and complaining. What a psycho."

"Hmmm, well, not too long ago, it was you we were dragging to the car to go off to college. Remember? And you insisted on bringing that goldfish of yours, too. What a pain."

"Poor Sparky," said Jane. "She hated being shuffled back and forth every time I came home for the weekend."

"Believe me, Sparky wasn't the only one who hated that." Vicky threw her daughter a dirty look. "I think I aged ten years when you were a freshman. Let's hope history doesn't repeat itself before Sophie graduates next year."

Jane's eye roll to her mother spoke volumes.

"Sophie, ten minutes," Tom yelled through the open front door toward his daughter's room upstairs.

"Coming. I'm saying goodbye to Booboo and Mrs. Baby." Leaving the family cats affected Sophie more than anything. For weeks she had showered the animals with treats, worried they would forget her. A few minutes later, Sophie stood by the car, wiping fresh tears from her high cheekbones. Her green eyes spilled over with emotion.

"Mommy, I miss them so much when I'm at school. And I'm so scared. The new roommates, all those classes in my major..."

"I know, baby. It's okay. You'll have a great time." Vicky wrapped Sophie in her arms and squeezed hard.

"Okay people, let's get this show on the road," Tom said. "Soph, do you have everything? Computer? Toothbrush? Pillow?" Sophie nodded. Tom turned and looked at his eldest. "Jane, are you riding along?"

Jane paused and looked at her sister and then to her parents.

Sophie's eyes pleaded for companionship. "Please?" she begged.

"All right. Let me grab my phone."

They drove away with Sophie crying, Jane texting and Vicky and Tom wondering what the next few months would bring for their family.

***

Tom looked forward to getting back to work at the nursery on Monday. They'd delivered Sophie to her college apartment and the flood of texts to Vicky indicated she loved her new roommates and having her own private bedroom. The weekend, filled with emotional upheaval and too much estrogen, left Tom exhausted and craving male companionship.

When he pulled into the Bumpkin parking lot on Monday morning, he spotted Walter climbing out of his truck. Tom perked up right away, anxious to hear what developed from Walt's meeting with the Stabs.

"Good morning," Tom called as he locked up the Benz SUV.

"Hey, Tom. Good morning to you. How'd you make out getting your girl back to school?"

"Eh, it was a little rough. But we'll be back up there in three weeks for parents' weekend."

"I had quite the meeting with the Stabs."

"No shit? What happened?"

The two walked into the store together after Tom entered the security code and unlocked the front doors.

46

"Well, after I got your text about adding a water feature, it gave me some good ideas to pitch, and they both love the fountain *and* a pond. Cha-ching!"

"Woo hoo!" Tom slapped Walter on the back. "I figured Mina would go gaga over the idea of having koi. You know, she always preferred the company of animals to humans."

Walter laughed. "True, man, very true indeed. Well, I told her we'd talk with our 'aquatic specialists' and get back to them with some preliminary drawings."

"Walt, that's great news. Hell, I can be your aquatic specialist. I'm ready to sock it to them. They're gonna get the most elaborate designs I can find."

"Dr. Stab is an odd bird, ain't he? I could've sworn he was already half-wasted by the time I got there at 10:00 in the morning." Walter laughed. "He's a real fancy boy, right? With his silk bathrobe and puffy slippers. Good God."

Both of them broke up laughing, picturing Dr. Stab pretending to be Hugh Hefner.

Tom straightened and tried to regain composure. "Okay. I'll start looking now for waterscape designs and let you know what I find."

Walter saluted Tom and started walking back outside. He paused and turned. "Speaking of water, I'm gonna go give some to our trees. They're dry as hell. I don't remember the last time we had any decent rain."

Tom whistled and walked into his office to start his computer. He brought up the Stabs' old account and studied the numbers again. They could afford to spend some serious cash. After all, they owned a shit-ton of property. He smiled thinking about the possibilities.

A knock on the door sent his good mood plummeting. He opened it to see Vicky smirking, standing next to Peggy. "Look who stopped in to say hello," Vicky said steering Peggy in Tom's direction.

"Jesus God. I mean, hi Peggy, it's uh... nice to see you," Tom stammered. Covering his tracks, he smoothed over his greeting. "So, what brings you in today?"

Vicky glared at him, knitting her brows into a frown.

"Lance sent me in to look for Halloween decorations," Peggy said. "As if I don't have enough problems. Jeez Louise."

Tom resisted a chuckle. "Is that right? Well, we've got a shit... I mean, we've got a bunch, over there." He pointed in the direction of a gigantic blow-up scarecrow under a Happy Harvest sign.

"He's always sending me on some wild goose chase these days. I don't know what to do." Peggy leaned in closer to Tom and continued, "His clients are leaving left and right. He screws up trades, forgets appointments. Then I'm stuck putting out the fires for him. I think he's got some sort of early dementia, you know? He started coming to the office in dirty clothes, and looks like he hasn't showered in a week." Peggy wrinkled her nose and waved a hand in front of her face.

"Ha! That's nothing new. He's always done that." Tom chuckled.

"Maybe. But I think it's gotten worse."

"No shit?"

Vicky frowned. "Tom."

"Yeah, yeah, okay." Tom shifted foot to foot, struggling to make conversation. "So what else is new?"

"My husband is driving me crazy. As usual," Peggy said. "Between him and Lance, and all of the kids' activities, I'm exhausted."

Dramatic as always. "So, Peggy," Tom interrupted, trying to change the subject. "What's going on in the office? Clients are leaving? Anyone I know?"

"Tom, you know I can't tell you that."

Ha! All of a sudden, Peggy is a paragon of virtue?

"Yeah, right." Tom sniffed and moved further away.

"So, I meant what I said the other day, Tom. You should consider coming back. Lance needs the help."

"Poor bastard." Tom grinned. "It's not a job for the faint of heart."

"Thomas!" Vicky looked angry now.

Clearing his throat, Tom continued, "That's nice of you to say, Peggy. But I've got my hands full here." He gestured to the store. "Despite the manual labor, I'm enjoying this."

"Hmm. Okay. Just sayin'. Clients still ask about you..."

Tom frowned and started to say something, but Vicky interrupted him. She grabbed Tom by the hand. "Okay, back to work for us. Thanks for stopping in to say hi. Let us know if you need help finding anything, okay?"

Vicky pulled Tom into the office and slammed the door. She pushed him into the office chair by his shoulders and leaned in close. "Don't you dare think about going back to Global Financial, Tom. Ever."

CHAPTER 8

With Jane and Sophie settled at college, life calmed down a bit. Although the nursery lost a lot of employees when the summer hires and college kids headed back to school, Vicky managed to fill the vacancies. She hired mostly part-timers, which saved the company a ton of money. No health insurance costs.

Walking into the house, Tom smelled something scrumptious cooking. Since buying the nursery he'd lost a good deal of weight and improved his fitness. Now, he enjoyed eating more without feeling guilty. "Hey babe, something smells great." Tom walked over to where Vicky stood stirring a big pot of spaghetti sauce on the stove. He planted a kiss on her cheek.

"Good thing I froze all that sauce I made last month," Vicky said. "After a long day at work, I'm wiped out. I forgot how hard it is to be on your feet all day. I'll be lucky if I don't pass out during dinner."

"I'm beat too. I'm gonna take a shower."

"Good, 'cause you stink." Vicky laughed.

After his shower, and ready to unwind, Tom headed to the fridge and grabbed a beer. He noticed a long strand of red tickets on the kitchen counter when he opened his Heineken. "What's up with the tickets?"

"Ah, those are for the raffle. It's tomorrow at lunchtime. I'll be heading over there around 11:30."

"You have to be there for the drawing?"

"It's one of those must-be-present-to-win contests. The Chamber is pushing for more memberships, so they invited the press to cover the event. They'll be giving out door prizes and whatever. WBOR will report on the winners, live as it unfolds. Ha!" Vicky waved her arms in the air in fake excitement. "Whoopie!"

"Well, you're the lucky one in the family. You should go. Take some of the flyers I printed out today about the sale." Tom rooted around in his briefcase and took out a stack of papers. "Here you go." Tom read aloud, "Fall perennial flower and outdoor furniture liquidation event at Country Bumpkin Nursery. Big sale! Big savings!"

Vicky chuckled. "Wow, so fancy. When do you think we can afford to hire a real advertising agency?"

Tom gathered his eyebrows together in a scowl. "Ha, ha, very funny, Vick." Grabbing the newspaper from the kitchen table, he walked over to the recliner in the den and chugged his beer. In seconds it was empty, then he looked at the time on his phone. In ten minutes, he'd get another. He turned on CNBC, muting it and watched the ticker at the bottom of the screen.

***

The next day, after discovering the Cray Chamber event included a free lunch, Tom decided to join his wife.

"Honestly, Tom, I doubt it'll be anything great." Vicky looked surprised he wanted to go along.

"Eh, I need a break. Walter can watch the shop while we go. Besides, I didn't even get very dirty today."

"Well, put on a clean shirt so you don't embarrass me." Vicky reached into the supply closet and grabbed one of their logoed shirts and tossed it to him.

After he changed clothes, they drove across town. Tom struggled to find a place to park in the jam-packed lot. "Jesus, look at all these cars. They better not be out of food already."

Vicky glared. "The drawings start at noon. It's only 11:30."

Frowning, he parked close to the back in one of the few remaining spaces, and they walked around to the front. Loud music thumped from a makeshift DJ booth set up outside, as people buzzed around vendor tables.

Once inside the building, everywhere he turned, Tom saw somebody he knew, including many of his former clients. Across the room he spotted his nemesis, Mina Stab and her plastic surgeon husband, Dr. Samuel Stab.

His first instinct was to lose himself in the crowd. But then he remembered Walter had met with them not long ago to discuss adding water features and some new landscaping ideas. "Vicky, come with me." He grabbed her hand and pulled her along as they wormed through the crowd. "We're going to say hello to the Stabs," he said as they neared the couple.

"What? Why?" Vicky stopped and pulled Tom toward her. "You're kidding, right?"

"No. Walter met with them about doing some new landscaping ideas, remember?"

"Yeah, okay." He dragged her along behind him.

Tom's pulse raced and for a moment he considered turning back. *No. Take the defensive stance. Surprise them.* "Mina! Sam! What a nice surprise to see you here." He stuck his hand out and shook Dr. Stab's hand. Both looked shocked to see their former financial advisor in a social setting.

"Hello, Thomas," Mina said, pulling off a pair of leopard print leather gloves and dropping them into a matching purse. "This must be your wife? I'm sorry, I don't remember your name." Mina looked down her nose at Vicky, scrutinizing her from multiple angles.

"Vicky, Mrs. Stab. It's nice to meet you." Vicky extended her hand and clasped Mina's soft, papery fingers.

Mina held on for a moment and peered closer. "Well, Thomas. Isn't she charming? How did you ever manage to snare such a pretty wife for yourself?" Everyone chuckled, except for Tom, who looked annoyed.

"Ha, ha. Very funny," Tom said, and then tried to change the subject. "I heard my employee, Walter, paid you a visit recently. To discuss some landscaping ideas?"

Dr. Stab piped himself into the conversation. "We've been unsatisfied with the landscapers we hired after Dennis died on our property." Dr. Stab looked to his wife for confirmation and she nodded. "And we had washed our hands of doing business with you. But there aren't any other options available. We'll have to make do with your little company."

Tom felt his face growing red. "Well, I certainly wasn't planning on—"

Vicky interrupted before he could finish, gripping his forearm tightly. A fake smile decorated her face. "We certainly weren't planning on seeing you both here today!" Her grip on Tom's arm remained firm. "I know we're excited to show you our landscaping ideas. Nice to meet you both." Vicky waved goodbye and pulled Tom away from the Stabs.

"Toodleoo," said Dr. Stab with a limp wave. Mina smirked.

"Those assholes," Tom said. "See, this is what I'm talking about. They're hateful."

"Yeah, you didn't exaggerate. That's for sure. But look! They're starting the raffle." Vicky and Tom inched their way closer to the stage. "Forget about them. I'm feeling lucky today."

Tom rolled his eyes following close behind her. Large crowds made him anxious, but he ignored the panic rising in his chest. He glanced at his watch and remembered it needed a new battery. Hopefully this wouldn't take too long and they'd serve lunch soon. His stomach growled in anticipation.

Everyone pulled out their raffle tickets and chattered, anxious for the winners to be announced. After a long-winded speech from the Chamber President, the staff began pulling winning tickets. All sorts of nice prizes, from gym memberships to restaurant gift cards and free movie passes. Ticket after ticket revealed the lucky winners, who screamed happily and ran on stage to claim their reward. With only the grand prize drawing left, Tom and Vicky figured they'd gotten skunked.

Tom patted his rumbling stomach, anxious to hit the chow line. "Let's head over and beat the crowd, Vick." He started moving away from the stage as the president pulled the final ticket number.

"637557," called the president. "That's our winning ticket! Who's our lucky winner?"

A hushed murmur ran through the crowd as hopeful players checked their numbers again.

"Okay, folks. I'll repeat the number," the president said. "637557. Anybody? Do we have a winner?"

Vicky whirled around and screamed, "Tom! I've got the ticket!" She jumped up and down, hugging him before taking off to claim her prize. "I have the winner!" she shouted as she ran through the crowd. Stunned, Tom stopped in his tracks and watched his wife ascend the stage.

The crowd clapped and cheered as the president handed Vicky a poster-sized explanation of her prize—four tickets on a luxurious ocean liner bound for a cruise to Central and South America in January. Photographers snapped pictures as Vicky beamed, waving to the crowd.

Within moments, Tom imagined himself on the deck of a large cruise ship, with the waves rocking him back and forth and the mist of salty ocean spray on his face. He pictured the sun high on the deck, kissing the sunning tourists with its rays, and flapping wet beach towels drying on deck chairs. His pleasant fantasies continued, plotting how wonderful it would be to escape the Pennsylvania winter for a brief respite and how he'd flaunt his tan at the Cray Country Club when he returned.

And then he remembered the inevitable. The common denominator with all the cruises he'd taken before. The one thing he feared he'd never escape—seasickness.

CHAPTER 9

From the moment Vicky won the contest, Tom's family talked of little else. Everyone obsessed about the upcoming trip, shopping for cruise-wear, stockpiling bathing suits, and researching the ports of call. Tom, not a fan of cruising, lacked their enthusiasm, but accepted he had little choice but to go along on the family trip. He realized Vicky's good luck would provide a once in a lifetime vacation. For free. So, he bit his tongue, drank too much beer, and stocked up on Dramamine.

Another perk surprised him after Vicky won the cruise. Now, on the cusp of the holiday season, people flocked to the Country Bumpkin for Christmas trees, lights and decorations to chat with Vicky about winning. Thanks to the Cray Chamber of Commerce, Tom's family not only won a cruise vacation, but enjoyed a serious uptick in their revenue.

So while his business thrived, and his family flourished, why wasn't Tom happy? Each morning, he stared in the bathroom mirror and asked himself, "Why? What am I supposed to do now? Better figure it out. Fast." With a week to go until Christmas, the Bumpkin bustled with customers. When he worked, Tom managed to push his negative thoughts away, but at night when he tried to get to sleep, his pessimism pecked at him, as it always had.

Some days at work he felt bone tired, the weeks of sleepless nights catching up with him. While Vicky closed the store, Tom stole away to his office to grab some alone time. After kicking off his work boots, he put his feet up on his desk and leaned back in his chair. He needed a minute to himself, without customers, employees or his wife bothering him about something. Grabbing a stack of mail from the corner of his desk, he perused the catalogs and bills, trashing some and tossing others into his pile of to-do work. Something caught his attention at the bottom of the stack. He got up and looked around before closing his office door. Then, he picked up the periodical and smoothed the shiny magazine's cover before he started to read.

Twenty minutes later, Vicky burst through the door. "Okay Tom. It's time to go h—" Her face lit up in anger, and she stormed over to the desk and yanked the magazine from his hands.

"What's this, Tom? You're reading *Financial Advisor* again? You know the doctor said you shouldn't be looking at this kind of stuff anymore. It's not good for you."

"Yeah, I know. But it's been so long, Vicky. I wanted to see the current trends. For *our* investments. Please. Give it back to me."

Vicky flung the magazine back in his direction, where it landed on the floor.

"Fine. I can't watch your every move. Let's go. We need to lock up before any other latecomer customers show up."

Tom scooped up the magazine with the stack of other mail and followed Vicky out as the alarm ticked its warning countdown. Vicky stood with arms crossed as she waited for him to unlock the car doors. Her body language signaled disgust, but he didn't care. He'd read whatever he damn well pleased.

***

The girls arrived home for the holidays, and cruise preparation moved into full throttle. Obsessed with their upcoming vacation, his family couldn't contain their excitement. Outnumbered, Tom threw in the towel, resigning himself to try to enjoy the trip. And to survive Christmas.

The holidays created ambiguous feelings for Tom. On one hand, he enjoyed seeing his family and friends at the Christmas parties, and other holiday celebrations. But seeing distant relatives, more specifically his in-laws, created a whole new level of stress.

Every December, Vicky's parents drove up from Florida and stayed with her older sister for a couple of weeks. They'd bully everyone to continue their boring Christmas Eve traditions like the Yankee gift swap game and singing carols. But this year, with Vicky winning the family cruise vacation, their time spent with his wife's relatives would be limited.

Every year, Tom made the same argument. "Vick, why does everything have to be at your sister's house?"

"You know how they are, Tom. They're obsessed with tradition."

"Yes, but even after they moved to Florida, they still manipulate the holidays. Does your sister get any say about this?"

"Tom, you know she'd love to let us take over, but as the oldest child, Mom and Dad think it's her duty to host all the family gatherings."

"Well, I'm surprised they don't force everyone to celebrate in Florida. They're so bossy."

"Yeah, they've hinted at that already."

Tom pondered celebrating the holidays in Naples, Florida, versus his sister-in-law's home in Harrisburg, Pennsylvania. At least at Vicky's sister's house he and his brother-in-law could drink beer in the basement man-cave. In Florida, despite the warmer weather, his wife's parents would be watching him like a hawk and counting his beers. And making him go to church.

So, Tom kept his mouth shut, sneaked in as many Christmas Eve beers as he could, and pretended to like the tacky gifts from Vicky's family.

This Christmas Eve proved no different. "Oh. Ice skates for the whole family," Tom said as Vicky opened the shared family present from the in-laws.

"We thought it sounded like something fun you could all do together," his mother-in-law said. "We got a great deal at a sporting goods store in Naples that was going out of business."

"Wonderful," Tom said. "I hope they fit."

Vicky threw Tom a dirty look. "Well, I'm sure if they don't, we can exchange them."

"Oh look, Vick." Tom pointed to the gift receipt. "All sales final."

***

With the perfunctory Christmas Eve gift exchange behind them, the Frye family headed home to unwind. The next morning, Sophie woke everyone early, her usual Christmas morning custom. They sipped coffee and opened presents.

"Parents, I'm going back to bed," Jane said. "It's too effing early for me."

"Me too," Sophie said. "Mom, wake me up at noon."

Vicky nodded in agreement. "Will do." She gathered wrapping paper from the floor, tossing it into the trash and then cozied up to Tom on the couch. She reached into the pocket of her bathrobe and pulled out a small box. Handing it to Tom, she planted a kiss on his cheek. "Merry Christmas."

"Vick, what's this?" Tom looked surprised.

"Oh, it's a little something for our trip."

"Really?" Tom ripped into the package and opened the box. "Wow. A watch!"

"It's waterproof, shatterproof and has all sorts of gadgets. You can count your steps, track your heart rate, answer your phone. All with the flick of the wrist."

"Thanks, babe. This is awesome. And much needed." Tom removed the watch from the packaging and strapped it on his wrist. "Very cool."

"Good. I'm glad you think so. But don't lose it." Vicky tousled Tom's hair and walked back to the kitchen, pouring herself a cup of freshly brewed Starbucks. "Do you want more coffee?"

Tom, looked up from tapping his watch, reading his vital statistics. "Uh, I'd better not. According to this, my heart rate is 114."

"Seriously? That's not good. Please don't have a coronary a week before our trip."

Tom laughed bitterly. "Yeah. God forbid you might have to cancel the big vacation." He leaned back into the couch and put his feet up on the coffee table.

Vicky folded her arms against her chest. "I'd only cancel if I couldn't find somebody to go in your place."

***

The morning of the trip, all the last-minute preparations had everyone scurrying around in a frenzy.

"So, everybody has their passports, correct?" Tom drilled his family at the breakfast table.

No one answered right away, glaring instead.

"Hello? People?" he repeated.

"Yes, for the billionth time, everyone has surrendered their passports." Vicky rose from her stool at the kitchen island and walked to the desk off the kitchen. She pulled all four passports out of the wooden box reserved for important things, like the checkbook. "They're here. Ready to go." She fanned them out like a winning hand of cards.

It was New Year's Day, and their evening flight and overnight in Ft. Lauderdale would be followed by an Uber ride to the port where they'd board their ship first thing the next morning. Two weeks on a cruise! Tom doubted his ability to survive the excursion, but he had no choice.

Sophie stretched, emptying the contents of her coffee mug in one large gulp. "You need to chillax, Dad."

"Hmmm," Tom said, storming out of the kitchen and grabbing his lunchbox off the counter. "Fine. I'm going to work. I need to make sure those part-time kids got the leftover Christmas trees out of the parking lot and marked down any remaining decorations for quick sale."

Vicky waved goodbye, fluttering her fingers. Tom heard the three of them giggling as soon as he closed the door. *Fine. Go ahead and laugh.* He leaned against the door, too tempted to forego eavesdropping.

Jane spoke first. "Okay, so is it my imagination, or is Dad getting weird again?"

"No, you're right. He's acting crazy. Mom?" He heard Sophie's footsteps followed by the sound of the Keurig brewing another cup of coffee.

"I admit, he does seem anxious," Vicky answered. "But I thought it might be the cruise. You know he's not a fan. The seasickness phobia?"

"But I saw he totally stocked up on Dramamine," Sophie said, "and those seasickness bands, and the patches to put behind your ear." Tom could hear a spoon clanging around a cup. No doubt Sophie had added a generous amount of half and half and stevia to her coffee.

"And how do you know that, miss?" Vicky's voice boomed. "Snooping again in our room? You know I hate when you do that, Soph."

Let her have it, Vick. The thought of their daughters poking around in his stuff made him queasy.

"I needed to find tweezers. I left mine at my apartment."

"God forbid the princess could go a day without tweezing," he heard Jane scoff.

"Mom! Why is she so hateful to me? Make her stop."

"Break it up, you two. I'm running to the store to get a few things for our trip."

Tom heard the sound of Vicky's keys, but the jingling stopped before she reached the garage door. He was ready to bolt, but when she continued speaking he couldn't resist listening further.

"Listen, girls. I am a little worried about Daddy. I caught him a couple of times watching MSNBC at the nursery. And I snagged him reading *Financial Advisor* again, too."

Vicky's voice got softer, so Tom leaned in closer to the door.

"I'm afraid he misses his old life. He complains more and more about being too old for manual labor, and how he didn't realize how good he had it before. Very negative comments."

"That's fucked up," Jane snorted. "We almost had to commit him right before he bought the Bumpkin."

"Language. Please. I need you both to be extra sweet to Daddy on this trip. Don't do anything to aggravate him. Okay?"

Tom wanted to hear the girls' reply, but apparently Vicky had other plans. She opened the door to the garage and because he'd been leaning in close, he nearly fell through to the kitchen.

"Tom?" she said. "I thought you'd left for the nursery." Her cheeks grew hot with embarrassment, realizing he must've heard the whole conversation.

"After I got in the car, I realized I forgot my glasses," he lied. "When I got to the door, I heard you all laughing. Jane's smartass comment about me being 'weird again,' so how could I resist?" His face fell, his eyes full of sadness. "I'm the brunt of everyone's jokes. Again." Tom stood to face his wife. "It's surprising what a little eavesdropping will tell you. Right, Vick?"

"Tom. I didn't mean to..."

"No, it's fine, Vick. Because you're right. I do miss it, working with my old clients. The excitement of the markets. I miss it all. I think I made a terrible mistake."

CHAPTER 10

"Come on, everyone, let's hustle! We've got to leave for the airport by 2:00." Tom buzzed around the house, alerting his family and assembling their luggage in the foyer. "I need to get these bags into the car ASAP. Girls, make sure you haven't forgotten everything."

"Daddy, I'm so tired," Sophie whined. "Why do we have to go so early? Our flight doesn't leave until 6:30."

Jane interjected, "Drink some coffee, princess. You'll feel better."

Vicky grabbed travel mugs and poured coffee for each of them. "Enough, Janie. Listen to Daddy and stop picking at your sister. Make sure we have everything. You can all take a cup to go." Vicky with Tom close on her heels, managed one last check on the family cats, Mrs. Baby and Booboo. "Isn't it nice that Peggy's taking care of the cats for us?"

Tom rolled his eyes. "Yes. I love the idea of her snooping through our house while we're traveling."

Vicky locked up and ushered the girls to the car.

"Boarding passes downloaded? Cruise tickets? Excursion vouchers? We got everything?" Tom started up the car while Vicky rummaged through her purse and carry-on bag, verifying each detail.

"Yep. Let's roll."

Two hours later they pulled into The Parking Spot, the off-site airport parking company Tom liked to use. They shuttled to the airport, sailed through security and waited for their flight. Unable to board, they entertained themselves and tried to pass the time.

Jane and Sophie both sported headphones, opting for music over conversation. Vicky and Tom glanced at their phones and surveyed the area. It looked like a full flight. Only a few scattered seats remained. Before too long, the flight attendants prepared to board the passengers for Ft. Lauderdale. Tom sniffed and tilted his head toward a lady with a mutt wearing an emotional support vest.

"Look at that. Why do people have to bring animals on a plane? It's too small as it is. It's ridiculous."

Vicky glared and whispered in his ear, "Hush, Tom. Don't start an altercation."

"Well for God's sake, the dog is way too big to sit on her lap. You watch. She's gonna get to butt ahead in line and board early because of the damn dog. And she'll end up in the bulkhead to boot. I should buy a dog to travel with. Just for spite."

The dog's owner, sitting within earshot, ruffled in her seat, recoiling from Tom across the aisle. The dog growled and barked once.

"Stop it. Please." Vicky grabbed his hand and squeezed.

"Okay, okay. I get it."

As predicted, dog lady boarded early, along with a host of families traveling with small children. What earlier appeared as a decent boarding assignment turned disappointing. The Fryes ended up in the back of the plane, three rows from the lavatories.

"See what I mean, Vick? We're screwed again. Stuck in the tail of the plane."

Tom continued to pout while he crammed his luggage in the overhead bin.

"Sir, would you like to put your suitcase under the plane?" the perky flight attendant asked, batting her false eyelashes.

"No, I would not." Tom stopped stuffing the carry-on and whirled around to face the attractive lady. "If I wanted to check my bags, I'd have done it earlier."

"Okay. No problem. Enjoy the flight."

"Yeah, right." He finished cramming the bags and sat down in the aisle seat, jostling the person in front of him. The seat's occupant, a burly bodybuilder swiveled around and scowled. "Sorry, man," Tom apologized. "How's it going?" The man turned around without answering.

"See that, Vicky. People can be so rude."

Vicky put in her earbuds and closed her eyes. Tom pouted and turned away.

***

"Sir? Sir? Something to drink?" The flight attendant returned with her notepad, taking drink orders.

"What? I was sleeping," Tom answered.

"Yes, I'm sorry. But it's a short flight. This is your only chance to order. Would you like something to drink or not?"

"Tom, answer the woman. Please," Vicky said.

"Okay, okay. I'll take a Heineken," Tom replied. "And a glass of water."

The flight attendant raised an eyebrow and looked to Vicky, stuck in the middle seat. "Diet Coke, please," she said. "Someone needs to stay sober."

The old lady seated next to Vicky ordered tomato juice.

"That's a weird thing to order on a plane, right?" Tom whispered to his wife. "Tomato juice? What if it spills? So messy. I hope she's not gonna get up and walk around while she has that drink."

"Keep your thoughts to yourself, Mr. Heineken." Vicky pulled down the tray table, moved the magazine from her lap and began reading.

Tom felt his cheeks grow hot. He put in earbuds and grabbed his iPad from the seat pocket in front of him. *Already she's bitching about the drinking.* "This *is* vacation, Vick." No response from his wife, only the side eye. "Fine. Ignore me." He browsed for something to watch on the airline's wi-fi.

After the flight attendants served the drinks and snacks, Tom dozed on and off. Periodically, he woke up as passengers stumbled into him on the way to the lavatory. He struggled to keep his mouth shut, even when tomato juice lady needed to use the bathroom twice. Rolling his eyes instead, he groaned inside. Despite the inconvenience of getting up from the aisle seat, it beat having to ask someone else to move. He liked the control and it kept him calm.

At one point, a twenty-something woman pushed her way down the aisle, dashing for the restroom as fast as she could. In her hand, she grasped the airplane barf bag, her face looking greener the closer she got. Tom panicked. *Oh my God. What if she barfs on me? I would freak out. Please, not that.*

"Did you see that, Vicky?" Tom nudged his wife as the woman slammed the bathroom door shut. "I hope you don't need to pee, because I bet she's barfing in there right now." He shuddered and looked to Vicky for comment. "Drunk, most likely. Trashed on the plane and getting sick. That's pathetic." Tom's voice tended to carry, even when he didn't want it to. Several passengers turned around, looking distressed.

"Let's hope she made it in time."

Jane and Sophie perked up too, nudging one another. "Dad. Please." Jane leaned across the aisle and tugged on his shirt sleeve. "You're acting like a jerk."

Tom crossed his arms and said nothing. In the meantime, the same annoying flight attendant barreled down the aisle toward the back of the plane. When the young woman emerged from the restroom, she asked, "Hey, are you okay? Feeling any better now?"

The passenger turned around, her face red with embarrassment. "Yes, thank you. My doctor thought I'd be over my morning sickness by now. Flying when you're pregnant is no picnic."

Ms. Flight Attendant, whose nametag read Wendy, smiled and patted her back. "Oh honey, don't be embarrassed! When I was pregnant with my three boys, I threw up every day for five months. You let me know if you need any help, okay?"

The new mother-to-be groped her way to the middle of the plane, hanging on to the backs of seats as she walked. A guy about her age, got up and scooted to the middle, relinquishing his aisle spot.

"Well, did you hear that?" Vicky said to her family. "Poor girl is expecting. So much for your theory, Tom."

"Yeah, smooth move, Sherlock Holmes," Jane said.

"Hahaha!" Sophie laughed. "I am beyond ready for this flight to be over. I can't wait to get on that ship!"

Jane nodded. "Truth. This plane is a petri dish."

Tom couldn't agree more. At least the cruise ships had hand sanitizing stations all over the place. Thank God. He sank lower in his seat and resumed watching *Bar Rescue* on his iPad. If he stayed on this plane much longer, he might need a tranquilizer. So, he distracted himself watching the syndicated reruns and stole Vicky's pack of pretzels when she went to the bathroom.

Tom found his groove and relaxed a bit, until the plane lurched and jolted him back to reality. Heavy turbulence rocked the 747. Audible gasps escaped several passengers. A baby seated on her father's lap a couple of rows ahead began to cry.

"Ladies and gentlemen, this is your captain speaking," interrupted a deep voice. "We're experiencing a little turbulence—in case you hadn't noticed." Clear and strong, the voice minimized the terrifying instability of the plane. "No need for concern, but please remain in your seats with your seatbelts fastened until we get out of this weather system. I'm trying to bypass a pesky thunderstorm, but we're on track to land on time at the gate. Thanks for your cooperation."

Worried passengers glanced among themselves. Tom noticed his daughters' eyes wide with surprise, and Vicky gripping the sides of her armrests. He knew she detested in-flight bumps as much as he did. The more the plane jostled and rocked, the more his anxiety catapulted. He forced himself to remember the psychiatrist's relaxation exercises. The deep breathing techniques worked, and mid-mantra Tom felt the plane land with a jolt and taxi to the jet bridge.

"Okay, now what?" Vicky asked Tom and the girls as they wheeled their suitcases through the airport.

"First thing I need to do is take a leak," Tom said. "No way in hell I'd go into that restroom after the pregnant chick blew her cookies."

Sophie pointed down the corridor. "Look, Dad. The bathrooms are over there."

"Thank God," Jane said. "My bladder's going to burst any minute."

Vicky nodded and pulled her luggage behind her. Ten steps later she tugged on Tom's sleeve, raising a pointed finger to a couple walking through the airport ahead of them. "Tom, don't freak out, but is that who I think it is?"

Tom stopped walking and pulled his glasses out of his pocket. His heart pounded in his chest. *Oh. My. God. No. It couldn't be possible. Could it?* He took off his glasses, rubbing them with his shirt before replacing them, but he couldn't deny it.

"Well?"

"Yep. It's them. Mina and Sam Stab."

CHAPTER 11

As he watched the Stabs weaving their way through the airport, Tom puzzled the irony. Coincidence? A cruel twist of fate? It irked him to think he couldn't escape his annoying former clients—and now landscaping customers—no matter where he went.

By the time his family finished at the restroom, the Stabs had disappeared. Thank God. He shrugged it off and figured he'd dodged a bullet.

Outside standing curbside at the airport, Tom scanned the rows of taxis and rental car buses. "Okay, now we need to look for the hotel courtesy van. Bright yellow." Tom checked his phone. "It said in our confirmation email that the driver would be waiting. Do you see it?"

"Not yet. Should we call?" Vicky asked.

"Over there, parental units. Could that be it?" Jane pointed to a chartreuse minivan. "The Hotel Snoozer Cruiser."

"Seriously, Dad? The Hotel Snoozer?" Sophie burst out laughing.

"I thought it was clever," Tom said, hailing the vehicle. "Come on. Let's walk over. He sees us."

After climbing into the van, the chatty driver got them to the hotel in record time. They checked in and got ready for bed.

"I doubt I'll get any sleep," Tom said.

"I'm so excited!" Sophie bounced up and down with anticipation.

"Stop with the bouncing, Soph," Jane said and smacked her sister with a pillow. "Why do we have to share a room? And a bed? I hate sleeping with her. She grinds her teeth."

"Shut up, Jane. Everyone get to sleep. Or at least try to." Tom turned off the light after pecking a kiss on Vicky's cheek. "All right, people. We're up at 6:30. Goodnight."

***

The next morning, they grabbed a quick breakfast and waited outside the hotel to catch a ride to the port.

"Here's our Uber, I think. Honda Pilot, right?" Tom said.

"Yes, Jamal is the driver's name." Vicky checked her phone to confirm the license plate.

Tom leaned in toward the open passenger window. "Hi, are you Jamal?"

The driver nodded and got out to help with their bags. "Going on a cruise, eh?"

"We sure are." Vicky smiled. "I won a contest. A trip for four to the Panama Canal."

"Yeah, I can't wait to dive into the unlimited drink package," Jane said, winking at her sister. "We're gonna have the best time. Ever."

Sophie nodded. "I know, right?"

Vicky peered over her sunglasses at the girls. "In the car. Now."

"Yeah, don't pretend like you're judging us, Mom. You'll be drinking along with me and Sophie. You know it. Dad too." Jane smiled. "For God's sake, people. It's a vacation. Loosen up."

"Jane, you're loose enough for all of us," Vicky answered laughing. "But you're right. Daddy and I haven't taken any real time off since we bought the Country Bumpkin."

"Daddy hates vacations," Sophie said. "He can never unplug and let go. Way too uptight."

"Truth," Jane agreed.

"Very nice," said the driver, an attractive middle-aged man with bushy black hair. "Good time of year to get away. But keep a close watch for pickpockets and beggars in the ports. Tourists make for easy pickings." He scratched his head. "Gotta pay attention all the time." He slapped his thigh and turned to Tom. "Keep your wallet in your front pocket, man." Then he pointed to the ladies and added, "Use crossbody straps with your purses, girls. Thieves are everywhere. Prey on tourists."

"Great." Tom climbed into the passenger seat of the vehicle. "At least you didn't mention kidnappers."

"Oh well, if you stick to the main tourist spots, you shouldn't have to worry about that too much. But keep your jewelry to a minimum, and don't attract too much attention." Jamal smiled when he saw the worried look cross Tom's face. "I just mean you don't want to look like stupid, rich Americans. No worries. There's a lot of great stuff to do, man. Windsurfing, fishing, visit the ruins, ziplining. You can even zipline at night now. Very cool."

"Wow!" Sophie said, nudging Jane. "We are totally doing that. Nighttime ziplining. My friend down the hall said she did that last year in San Jose and saw all kinds of cool animals. Cougars, snakes, bats, hanging out in the trees when you zip by."

Jane looked skeptical. "Yeah, I don't know. We'll see."

"Sounds terrifying," Vicky said.

"People, let's not get carried away. First we need to get to the damn ship." Tom looked at his watch, agitated and fidgeting in the passenger seat. "How long till we get to the port, chief?"

"Ten minutes," Jamal answered. "No sweat. You'll make it in plenty of time."

Yeah, I've heard that before. If they missed getting on the ship, there'd be hell to pay.

"I hope you're right. It's only two hours until we sail."

The Uber driver picked up speed. "Easy peasy, mister."

***

73

"All right. That's enough, ladies," Tom said rooting around in his backpack. "Vick, is it too early to put on one of those seasickness patches?"

"Why don't you hold off until we board the ship?"

"Fine. But I'm putting on one of these wristbands." He pulled out a bag of plastic bracelets guaranteed to ward off seasickness and offered them to his family. "Here. You should all put these Sea Bands on while we wait. One for each wrist."

"I read about these," Jane said. "They use acupressure to combat the nausea, right?"

"Yep. Let's hope they work. Here Vick, pick out your favorite color." He tossed the bag over to his wife. "I left the red ones for you."

"Thanks, honey, but I don't get seasick. I'll take my chances." She threw the bag back at Tom and smiled.

"Okay, but don't come crying to me when you're barfing off the deck." He put the remaining Sea Bands back into his pack.

Daunting long lines snaked through the cruise terminal separating the masses of people. Dozens of uniformed cruise employees bustled among passengers, checking boarding documents and directing people to the correct line.

"Welcome to the Oceanos, Mr. and Mrs. Frye," a perky blonde said upon reading Tom and Vicky's boarding literature. "We're so excited you're here with us. Congratulations on winning the grand prize in the contest."

Tom and Vicky exchanged a surprised look. "Thanks," Vicky said. "We're thrilled to be here."

"Great, let me point you in the right direction." The woman took Vicky by the elbow, guiding her past the long lines of anxious passengers. "Celebrity boarding is over here," she said and made a sweeping gesture toward a swanky reception area.

"Celebrity boarding? What the hell is that?"

"Tom! Stop!" Vicky blushed and gave him a stern look. "Thank you," she said, looking at the woman's nametag. "Thanks, Erin."

"My pleasure," Erin replied. "Enjoy the champagne reception."

"OMG, I love this," Jane said, nudging Sophie. "Let the day drinking commence."

"Jane, enough," Tom grumbled. "Let's go get checked in."

A gentleman in a crisp white uniform scanned their boarding documents and opened a roped entrance to the reception area.

"Have fun!" Erin called as she waved goodbye. "Take lots of pictures!"

Tom turned and waved an unenthusiastic response. "Yeah, yeah," he said under his breath.

The small, efficient line moved along, and soon the Fryes found themselves whisked away to a private reception for customers with exclusive cabins. Champagne, tropical cocktails and mouth-watering canapes circulated via attractive waitstaff as the elite waited to embark. Although impatient, Tom chugged a couple of beers and enjoyed the smoked salmon.

Twenty minutes later, a cruise ship employee ushered everyone down a long hallway and instructed passengers to have their boarding documents ready. Embarkment time had arrived. Tom got his first look at the Oceanos and it took his breath away. He had forgotten how huge these cruise ships were when you walked next to them.

"Wow! Look at the size of her!" Vicky said.

Sophie and Jane jumped up and down with excitement.

"It's massive," Tom agreed.

As they walked, the ship's photographer called them over for a photo. Tom grumbled but went along with it anyway, and they posed for a couple of pictures. At the gangway entrance, the cruise line representative scanned their documents into the system and took individual photos. They'd made it onto the ship at last.

As a family, they'd been assigned a luxurious ocean-front suite with two bedrooms, two bathrooms and private balcony. Tom thought it sounded too good to be true, and as a skeptic, he figured they'd been scammed. He waited on deck and watched passengers filing in. While Vicky chatted with the girls, he walked to the starboard side of the Oceanos and pretended to look out onto the water. Checking over his shoulder to make sure his family wasn't looking, he pulled out his phone, opening up the stock application. Good. The DOW was up 172 points. An excellent way to start vacation.

He put his phone back in his pocket when he saw Vicky hustling in his direction.

"What are you up to over here by yourself?"

"Nothing. Just feeling a little antsy. You know, all this hurry up and wait crap." He smiled and pulled his sunglasses down from the top of his head to hide his eyes. Vicky saw right through him most of the time.

"Tom, when do we need to turn our phones off?" She took her cell out of her bag and did a cursory glance. "It'll be strange to disconnect from everything on this trip."

"Yeah, well. You won't have to worry about that, hon."

"Why? What do you mean? You said the internet fees were too pricey."

"I did, but that was before I knew they included wi-fi in your prize winnings." He grinned and patted the phone in his shirt pocket. "Score."

"Well, the girls will be ecstatic. Sophie has complained non-stop about being cut off from the world."

"I thought it might be fun not to share that news. At least, not yet anyway." He smirked and chuckled a bit.

"Tom, that's cruel. You can't do that." But she stifled a grin.

"Think of it as an experiment in social media deprivation." Tom could tell when Vicky tried her best not to laugh.

"Okay. But not the whole trip? We'll all end up suffering if they can't text for two weeks."

"Yeah, I know. Forty-eight hours. Tops. I promise." He grabbed Vicky's hand and smiled, steering her toward the bar. "Let's go get another cocktail."

They grabbed drinks from the bartender and Tom spotted Jane and Sophie talking to some sketchy looking guys. *Great. The ship hasn't even left the port.*

As he and Vicky walked across the deck toward them, a loud wave of feedback pierced the air, causing everyone to stop what they were doing. Passengers looked from one to another, searching for the source of the noise. Soon a tall man with highlighted spikey blond hair and a dark tan slid across the deck toward the crowd. He smiled and tapped a portable microphone with his finger.

"Attention, everyone! Attention! Hello, cruisers! I'm your Cruise Director, JJ!" He walked through the crowd, smiling and waving, blowing kisses to the ladies. "Okay, cruisers, now it's your turn to say hello to me. Go on." He held the microphone up to the crowd and waited for their response.

"Hi, JJ," a few of the passengers said together.

"Oh, come on, people. You can do better than that. Again!"

"Hi, JJ," came the slightly louder response.

A few people snickered. Tom's eyebrows drew together in annoyance. He leaned closer to Vicky and whispered, "Jesus. Are we gonna have to deal with this joker for the whole trip? Already I can't stand him."

"Shhh, Tom. I can't hear."

Tom frowned but stopped talking.

"Okay, cruisers. It's time. Everyone follow me to the upper deck for the Muster Drill." JJ reached behind the bar and retrieved a long pole with a yellow flag attached to the top. He raised it into the air, waving it back and forth.

"Ha. It looks like a golf course flag," Tom said, loud enough for a couple of passengers to turn and stare at him.

Vicky looked irritated. Meanwhile, a loudspeaker announcement blared, inviting all the passengers to assemble at the muster station on the fourth deck.

"Okay, follow me. Single file. After we take care of business, the fun will begin." JJ led the group using the flagpole as a baton.

The muster drill lasted only ten minutes once it finally got going, and Tom did his best to ignore the annoying perky deckhands demonstrating how to put on lifejackets and lower the tender.

"I'd like to throw Rod Stewart and his friends overboard in that dingy," Tom whispered to Vicky. "Without any flotation devices." He chuckled when he saw her lips quivering. She smacked his hand and tried to concentrate on the demonstration.

When the drill wrapped up, the Oceanos made its way out of Port Everglades toward the open sea. Tom looked down at his wrists and prayed. "I hope these Sea Bands work."

Vicky smiled and hugged him. "We'll know soon enough, won't we?"

Before too long, a man dressed like a butler appeared. "Follow me, please. Your stateroom is now ready."

"About time," Tom said.

The room did not disappoint. It looked much like the ship's website photos they'd pulled up online after Vicky won the contest. Large spacious rooms decorated with comfortable, plush furniture, a tasteful kitchen breakfast bar with leather stools and multiple flat-screened televisions mounted throughout. Both bedrooms featured king-sized beds and attached private baths. And the highlight, the balcony, afforded a clear view of blue sky and open water with cushioned chaise lounge chairs. The suite made the cabins from his previous two cruises look as if they'd been crafted from converted freighter ships.

The family, too excited to unpack anything, left to explore the ship. Tom realized the opportunity to carve out a little time for himself. He headed out to the private veranda to relax.

"You ladies have fun. I'm gonna take a little nap on these lounge chairs."

"Okay, Daddy. See you soon." Sophie waved goodbye.

When he heard the cabin door close and knew for certain Vicky and the girls had left, he raced to his suitcase on the luggage rack. He rooted around until he found what he wanted, pulling out the stack of magazines and running his thumb over the glossy covers of *Medical Economics, Financial Advisor Today,* and a few other articles and charts he'd printed out at the Bumpkin. Tom scooped them up and hustled out to make himself comfortable. He stationed a cold beer on the table to his right, and stacked the reading materials on the ottoman.

God, I miss this. All of it. The excitement of the markets. The stock analysis portfolios and helping clients achieve their goals. But that's over. Right? Or is it?

CHAPTER 12

Tom read for a long time on the deck, enjoying the ocean air and cool breezes while he drank a few beers, and then fell asleep listening to a podcast, *Planet Money* from NPR.

When he woke, the sunset dipped along the horizon, and Vicky and the girls hadn't gotten back yet. Feeling concerned, he gathered up his reading materials, threw on his flip flops and left to go look for them.

After an afternoon of drinking beer and reading in the sun, Tom felt groggy and disoriented. Without Vicky and the girls, he recognized the old stirrings of anxiety fluttering in his stomach. *Well, you could've gone with them. You chose to stay in the cabin and read your contraband.*

The ship glided along without a lot of turbulence, thank God, and the wrist Sea Bands appeared to work. So far. Everywhere he looked, people smiled and laughed, enjoying cocktails and conversation. He scanned the crowd for his family but didn't spot them.

JJ the Cruise Director entertained a group of single women at the bar with his antics and stories and they hung on his every word. His follow-the-leader flagpole remained stationed beside his bar stool. *What a life that joker has. Hang out in your bathing suit all day and hit on pretty women in bikinis.*

Tom searched the bars and the swimming pool decks and decided to treat himself to another beer while he looked. *Might as well use that bottomless drink package. Right?*

As he turned away from the bar to continue his search, he spotted Vicky and the girls near the exit door, talking to a tall woman in a leopard-print bathing suit. As he got closer, he gasped and stopped in his tracks. She looked familiar. Blonde bob, dripping in glinting, gold jewelry. Beside the woman was a chubby man in a long white beach robe and purple flip flops. Then he knew. It was the Stabs. Of all the luck, how could this have happened? How could they have booked the same cruise?

Panicked, Tom wondered how to escape without talking to them, but where would he go? Vicky spotted him and started waving, calling him over. He took a deep breath and joined them.

"Look who I ran into at the pool," Vicky said.

"Well, well, Thomas. There you are. What have you been doing? Sleeping the whole afternoon away?" Mina stuck her hand out to shake Tom's.

"Hello, Mina. Sam." Tom reached out to shake hands while averting his eyes from the purple flip flops. "Fancy meeting you here. There goes the neighborhood."

"Tom." Vicky grabbed his hand and gave it a firm squeeze. "Isn't this a nice surprise?"

"Yes, indeed. Quite a surprise."

"Frankly, if we'd have known you'd be on this cruise, we would've booked elsewhere," Mina said. "Isn't a cruise of this caliber out of your price range?" She sniffed and then continued. "Oh, that's right. It's free. Your wife won the contest. How fortunate."

Jane rolled her eyes and elbowed Sophie. "We're going back to get cleaned up for dinner." The girls turned, waving in the direction of the Stabs. "Bye. Nice meeting you both."

Tom raised his hand and winked to the girls. "Later."

"Goodbye, yourself," Mina said as the two hurried off.

"For real," Sophie said giggling as she and Jane walked away.

Mina and Sam continued to stare at Tom and Vicky, as if they expected an explanation. An awkward silence fell over the foursome.

"So, first dinner tonight," Vicky said, breaking the silence. "I for one am very excited! We're seated at the Captain's table."

"*Humph*," Dr. Stab blurted out. "How did you manage that, Tom?"

Vicky intervened. "It's all part of the prize package, Dr. Stab. One of the perks along with the unlimited drink packages and off-shore excursions, including dinner at the Captain's table every night—unless we opt for one of the other restaurants. Those are included in our prize, too. We've heard great things about the food on this cruise line."

"It's top-notch," Dr. Stab agreed, "and one of the reasons we choose to sail on Fairy Tale Cruise Lines." He turned toward his wife. "Mina refuses to travel on any other line."

"Why would we go elsewhere? They *know* us," Mina defended.

"I'm sure," Tom said, as sarcasm dripped from his voice.

Mina tugged on her husband's sleeve. "Samuel, darling, we must go visit with JJ. I'm sure he's wondering where we are."

"Right you are, darling. How rude of us."

Tom chuckled. "JJ? The flaky cruise director guy? With the highlighted hair and golf flag?"

"I beg your pardon," Mina scowled. "Whatever do you mean by that?"

"Well, look at the guy," Tom said. "He looks like a combination of Rod Stewart and Richard Simmons."

"How dare you insult my nephew?" Mina's eyebrows knitted together in angry arches over her eyes.

"What? You're kidding right? That guy is your nephew?" Tom laughed out loud.

"I couldn't be more serious. And I demand you apologize. He's a wonderful young man."

"Yes, Tom. Apologize this instant," Vicky said.

Tom stammered, "Y-y-yeah, sure. I apologize. Sorry."

"I'm appalled you'd criticize someone you haven't even met." Mina's arms were crossed, foot tapping with impatience. "Your apology doesn't sound sincere."

"Well, I think we said hi, I mean—"

Tom opened his mouth again, but Vicky cut him off. She grabbed Tom's hand and pulled him close. "It's been lovely to see you, but we should get ready for dinner. We're in the early seating."

"How vulgar," Mina said. "We cannot possibly eat before 9:00 P.M."

"Lucky for us, I guess," Tom whispered close to Vicky's ear. But the look on Mina's face revealed she'd heard the comment.

Dr. Stab raised his hand in a limp wave goodbye.

"Enjoy your trip," Tom called as he and Vicky slipped away. When they were out of earshot Tom started his rant. "Of all the people to run into on this trip. Seriously? Is there no God?"

Vicky chuckled. "I know. I mean, what are the odds? But it's a big ship, Tom. Hopefully we won't run into them again. We'll check out the other pools."

"Yeah, I guess." Tom rummaged in his pocket for the key to the suite. "I could use another drink."

"Amen to that," Vicky said.

He moved to the room fridge, taking out some Chardonnay and poured a glass for each of them.

"Cheers." He clinked glasses with Vicky.

"Cheers to you." She took a sip. "Could be a long night. Let's hope we don't run into the Stabs again."

"Yeah, or anybody else we don't want to see. God knows who else is on this ship." He chugged his wine in a few gulps, setting the glass on the bar. "I'm hitting the shower. Then I'm getting a refill. Pre-game!"

Vicky swirled her wine glass and took another small sip. "Oh boy, here we go."

CHAPTER 13

Tom squinted as he made his way into the main dining room, shielding his eyes from the glittering crystal chandeliers and shiny brass fixtures. His brain hummed and buzzed with the undercurrent coursing through his body. The energy in the room, palpable and contagious, sucked him in like a vortex.

Vicky's face looked flushed when she tugged on his arm. No doubt influenced by the happy hour cocktails and excitement. "Oh. My. God. I cannot believe this." She took in the detail of cascading stairways leading up to a second tier of dining, with crystals sparkling from every surface.

"Holy shit!" Jane elbowed Sophie. "This is unbelievable."

"Even better than the pictures on the website. Jane, let's find our table."

The family needed no further help, intercepted by the maître d' as they cruised past his post.

"May I help you?"

"We're the Frye's. Early seating," Tom said, clearing his throat.

"Ah. But of course. My apologies, madam," the man sputtered, turning his attention to Vicky and ignoring Tom. "One of our celebrities. Forgive my oversight." He bent at the waist, taking Vicky's hand and planting a kiss on it. "Please follow me to the Captain's table." He extended his arm and Vicky accepted as they strolled to an elaborate table for eight with a spectacular ocean view.

Sophie and Jane rolled their eyes. Tom pouted all the way to the table.

"Madam," the maître d' cooed as he pulled out the chair for Vicky.

"Oh hehe, thank you." Vicky looked up from her seat to read his nametag. "Thank you, Antoine." She giggled and gave him a tiny wave as he pulled out chairs for Jane and Sophie as well. Tom stood, waiting his turn, but Antoine merely glared and bowed farewell to the ladies.

"Well, that was rude." Tom pulled out his own chair and tossed his cell phone on the table with a loud thump. "What a jerk."

"Tom," Vicky said. "Calm down."

"Chill, Daddy," Sophie said. "Why don't you have a drink?"

"Excellent idea, sis," Jane agreed. "Tonight, we get wasted."

The girls laughed, clinking their water glasses in a toast.

Tom frowned. "Hmm, I hope you two are going to behave yourselves. And don't get into any trouble." He cleaned his glasses with the napkin from his place setting, moving the silverware around in clanking, choppy motions. "I saw you were already on the prowl for boys. Caught you talking to a couple of clods by the pool."

"So what?" Jane said. "We're adults. We can do what we want."

"Yeah, well then be prepared to bail yourself out of jail if you get in trouble." He scowled at his family, lowering his voice before continuing. "And no funny stuff. No smoking pot. I mean it. I don't want our vacation turning into some kind of international incident." Tom sipped from his water glass and continued, "And absolutely, no bringing men back to our suite. You need to be extra careful. People may not be what they seem."

Vicky shifted her gaze from the girls to Tom. "Yes, dear. Oh, but look! The captain is coming over to the table. Behave, everyone."

"Whoop de doo," Tom said, twirling his pointer finger in the air and smirking.

"Good evening, I'm Captain Cosmo Bligh." The man bowed, sweeping his right arm out wide as he folded his left behind his back. His crisp, white uniform bristled when he moved.

Tom stood to shake hands. "Tom Frye. My wife, Vicky, and our daughters, Jane and Sophie." Tom gestured to each member of his family during the introduction.

"It's a pleasure to meet you all. Welcome to the Oceanos." Captain Bligh smiled, his blue eyes twinkling. He met Vicky's gaze and held it for a moment too long, bending down and kissing her hand. "Madam. Charmed." The thick British accent irritated Tom immediately.

"Oh," Vicky said and giggled. "My pleasure, Captain."

"I believe you can release my wife's hand now."

"Ah yes, of course." The captain let go of Vicky's hand and straightened. "Well, I must introduce myself at a few other tables. I'll be back momentarily. The rest of our tablemates should be here imminently." He smiled at Vicky. "Please excuse me."

Vicky fluttered her fingers again in a wave goodbye as they watched the man stop at a nearby table. Tom noticed a blush creeping across his wife's cheeks.

"Well, isn't he a slimy bastard?"

"Tom! Lower your voice."

"My voice is fine. Honestly, Vick, you could act a little less excited by this joker. So, he's a captain. Big whoop. And did he say his name was Captain Bligh? Like from *Mutiny on the Bounty*?" Tom groaned. "What a phony. That's gotta be made up. Right?"

"You're acting crazy, Tom. I'm sure that's his name. If that's what he said." Vicky ran her fingers through her hair. "To be honest, I'm not one hundred percent certain. All I heard was Captain Cosmo..."

"Oh, right. You practically swooned, Vick. Unbelievable."

"Parental units, please," Jane said. "Don't cause a scene."

"Oh, hush up, Jane," Vicky chided. "And you too, Sophie. Before you open your mouth to comment."

"Well, I'm insulted," Sophie said. "The lady doth protest too much, Mother."

"Enough, people," Jane said. "Someone's coming over to our table with Antoine."

"*Humph*," Tom grunted. "Fine. I could use someone to spend time with other than Captain Smooth Talker."

"Well, I'm glad you feel that way, honey," Vicky said. "Because the Stabs and JJ are headed straight for our table."

CHAPTER 14

"Oh, come on." Tom rolled his eyes. "This can't be happening."

"Well, look who it is." Dr. Stab guided Mina to her seat and pulled out the chair. "Oh, right. I forgot we'd be seeing you at the Captain's table."

"I beg your pardon?" Tom stood and turned to face the Stabs.

"Tom. Stop," Vicky said under her breath. "Hi again. So nice to see you."

"Indeed," Mina said. "I take it you've met our nephew, JJ? JJ, have you met the Frye family? Mrs. Frye, uh, Nicky? She won the cruise from the Chamber of Commerce."

With a beaming smile, JJ stood behind the Stabs, waiting to take his seat. He looked stoned, his eyes glassy and shining.

"It's Vicky, Mrs. Stab," his wife said patiently.

"Hi, hi, hi," JJ waved and twirled around like a ballerina. "Oh, how fun this will be. Auntie, you didn't tell me you and Unkie Sam had friends on the cruise."

"Yes, well. Tom Frye was our financial advisor until a few years ago. Now he's our landscaper."

"No way. Fabu! Talk about a career change, right?"

"W-w-well, it didn't exactly happen the way Mina described it," Tom stammered. "You see, I was a financial advisor with Global International. Sam and Mina were long-time clients. About five years ago I decided I needed a change. Bought a landscaping company. My wife, *Vicky* and I own it together."

"Yes, it's been quite a challenge. I mean, Tom and I had never worked together before, so—"

"That's a dynamite story," JJ interrupted. He turned his attention to the girls. "Remind me again who these charming young ladies are..."

"Hi, I'm Jane. And this is my sister, Sophie." Both girls giggled.

"Enchantreresse, ladies." JJ jumped up from the table and bowed. "Are you of legal age?" His eyes did a quick assessment.

"Close enough," Sophie said.

"You don't say?" JJ cooed. A wry smile slid across his face.

Mina cleared her throat and Dr. Stab guzzled a sip from his cocktail while an awkward silence hung in the air. A few minutes later, the Captain returned, nodded hello to everyone and introduced himself to the Stabs. He waved over a server who took drink orders and rattled off the evening dinner menu choices.

"By the way, Captain, Mina and Sam are my aunt and uncle."

Dr. Stab smiled like a proud, doting father and blew up like a tick. "Yes. JJ is my sister Sally's only son."

The Captain acted amused. "Well, is that so? It is a small world, isn't it?"

The table nodded in agreement. A few seconds ticked away until Tom broke the ice.

"So, Mina," Tom hesitated. "I thought you said you couldn't eat before 9:00? How'd you end up in the early dinner service?" He smirked and leaned back in his seat.

"Oh, I'm afraid that was my fault," JJ said. "I told Auntie and Unkie that as a staff member, I'm delegated to the early seating." He looked over and smiled at Mina, who patted his hand. "They were sweet enough to agree. They're the best."

Dr. Stab reached behind Mina's chair to tap JJ gently on the back. "Anything for our JJ."

The table exchanged collective eye rolls, and Captain Bligh, tired of the conversation, turned to Vicky and asked about the contest.

"As Captain of this fine ship, I'm assigned the late seating. Most of the time, anyway. But given the circumstances... I mean honoring you, and your early dinner seating, I deferred. By the way, how did you win this trip, again, Vicky? May I call you Vicky?"

"Oh, sure," Vicky said. "Well, it's a long story."

"Mrs. Frye is good with me." Tom looked annoyed.

"I beg your pardon?" Captain Bligh said.

Vicky threw Tom a cautionary look before continuing, "Please, ignore my husband. As I was saying..." She summarized for Captain Bligh how she had entered and couldn't believe her luck in winning the grand prize.

"So, that's how we came to be here," Vicky concluded.

"Yay us," Jane said.

"Hehehe," Sophie added. Several moments passed before she could stop laughing.

"Seems as though someone is having too much fun," JJ said as he pointed to the empty cocktail glasses lined up in front of the Frye girls. "Make sure to pace yourselves, darlings. That's my advice. The real fun happens after dinner."

"Word," Jane said.

"I need a drink," Tom said, leaving his seat at the table and heading for the bar.

"I'll join you." Vicky grabbed Tom's hand and they walked off.

As they made their way outside the dining room to the closest lounge, Tom sighed and ran a hand through his hair. He stopped and turned to his wife. "How in the hell am I going to be able to sit with these clowns at dinner every night? I mean, the Stabs. That's bad enough, but their kooky nephew and the sleazy captain? It's too much."

"Tom, don't you think you might be overreacting? The Stabs and JJ are strange, but Captain Bligh seems nice enough."

"Nice? Nice? Yeah, sure. He's nice all right. To you. Too nice, in fact."

"Oh, come on, Tom. You're not jealous? Of the captain? He's harmless. Besides, he's too old for me." She smiled, teasing, but Tom stopped and whirled around to face her.

"He's too old? So, if he was a young, dashing Navy captain you'd ditch me? Throw me overboard?"

"Don't be ridiculous. You're being silly now."

"I'm not. I'm not jealous—and I'm not overreacting. That guy is flirting with you big time. I don't like it one bit."

Vicky ignored his remarks and moved up to the bar. "Hi, could I have a glass of chardonnay, please?" She held up the wrist band that guaranteed the unlimited drink package.

"Certainly, ma'am," the bartender said. "But, you know, your server in the dining room could've gotten you whatever you wanted."

"Yes, I'm aware. My husband needed a little air."

The bartender nodded and looked at Tom. "For you, sir?"

"Tequila. On the rocks. Splash of lime juice. Please."

"Yes, sir."

"Oh, boy. It's gonna be a long night." Vicky let out a long sigh.

Tom and Vicky returned to the table just as the waiter served the salad course. It appeared their absence had relieved some of the earlier tension. Captain Bligh and JJ were entertaining everyone with stories from a cruise to Alaska where they had to quarantine an entire floor of the ship after a nasty outbreak of norovirus.

"Yes, it was unfortunate. Even the passengers who weren't sick had to stay on their floor, but it was the only way to contain the outbreak." Captain Bligh shrugged and continued in his smooth, accented voice, "We did our best to keep everyone comfortable until we got into port, but they turned out to be a cranky lot."

"Yes, a couple of rogue passengers tried escaping. We had to station guards by all the exits." JJ and the Captain chuckled, but the rest of the table looked horrified.

"Dude, so, you held them hostage?" Jane asked.

"Not hostage, princess," JJ said. "It was for the common good."

"I'd flip the eff out," Jane said. "Like, that's my worst nightmare. Quarantined on a ship with a bunch of randoes barfing their brains out."

"Hahaha," Sophie laughed.

"That's enough, Jane," Tom said. "Thank you for your comments. Say, Captain Bligh, not to change the subject, but are you related to *the* famous Captain Bligh?"

"As a matter of fact, I am. Distant relative on my father's side."

"Fascinating. Does that mean you're a member of the Australian Navy?" Vicky asked.

"Yes. Until I retired eight years ago."

"Australian, huh?" Tom knew Captain Bligh's accent would grate on his last nerve by the end of the cruise. *Figures. Smarmy Aussie bastard.*

Dinner entailed many courses, and lots of awkward conversation. The table imbibed throughout, with the waiter running for refills of tropical drinks for the girls, wine for the ladies and Bankers Club for Dr. Stab. Tom stuck with his tequila, and JJ and the captain hoisted a steady stream of specialty drinks decorated with pineapple spears and dark rum floating on top.

While Captain Bligh blathered on about his family history and flirted with Vicky, Tom grew incensed and frustrated. *Ah, this is the perfect opportunity to annoy Mina. She looks irritated and jealous since she's not in the spotlight.* "So, Captain, we appear to have a diverse table here." He paused for effect, gesturing out to the members of the table. "Did you know Mina is Swedish?"

Mina perked up after hearing her name. "Yes. I am."

"Isn't that interesting?" Captain Bligh looked uninterested.

"Yes, in fact, Mina is so devoted to her homeland, she once tasked me to invest in Swedish companies for her." Tom paused and swirled his cocktail. "Isn't that right, Mina? Remember? You wanted to buy stock in Swedish Fish? Hahaha! Swedish Fish, the candy. Get it?"

Dr. Stab's eyebrows raised as he turned toward his wife. "What's your point, Tom?" He took a large slurp from his glass.

Tom smirked. "My point, Sam, is that she thought the candy was Swedish because of its name. It's made in Canada somewhere. By Cadbury."

"Are you making fun of me, Thomas? Because I don't find that amusing in the least." Mina stood up from the table, throwing her napkin on her chair. "Sam, it's time we went back to our suite. I've had more than enough for one evening."

Dr. Stab, the captain and JJ all stood.

"Goodnight Auntie. Unkie. Toodles." JJ kissed Mina on both cheeks, European style, and shook hands with his uncle. The Stabs left without saying a word.

"So, if Swedish Fish are made in Canada," JJ said, "does anyone know where Belgian chocolate is made?"

"Umm, Belgium, I think," Jane said.

"Imagine that," Sophie chimed in.

"And I think it's time to say goodnight," Captain Bligh added and headed off to greet more of his fan club.

"I couldn't agree more," Vicky said. "It's been quite a night."

"Word." Jane turned to Sophie and added, "Time to prowl."

"For real," Sophie said. "Let the games begin."

Only Tom remained at the table, nursing his drink. God only knew what would happen on this trip. He hoped he'd make it out sane. He noticed that JJ had lagged, waiting for the girls. Probably harmless, he figured.

Too bad he heard JJ whisper a little too loudly, "Hey, ladies, want to smoke a joint?"

CHAPTER 15

By the third day of sailing, Tom longed to set foot on land again. He obsessed over replacing the sea sickness patches and the Sea Bands bracelets, double and triple checking the package information to make sure he used them correctly. Seasickness terrified him. But he tried hard to make the best of the experience. He woke up anxious to see the first port of call. Avoiding the Stabs remained his number one goal, but he wanted to enjoy this vacation.

"Good morning, family," he said, opening the doors to the girls' bedroom.

"What time is it?" Sophie sat up in bed.

"It's too effing early to be awake, that's what time it is," Jane mumbled.

"Get up, ladies. Today's the first shore excursion. We disembark in an hour."

"Where are we, Tom? I forget our first stop."

"Colombia, Vick. Cartagena. I can't wait to get off this ship and walk around."

"Word," Jane said. She turned to her sister. "Beach time. All day."

"Just make sure you keep an eye on the clock, girls. We need to be ready to come back to the ship at 3:00."

"Well, by then Jane will be fried to a crisp. So that should work." Sophie stretched out a suntanned leg, revealing golden brown skin. "I plan on winning the tanning contest. As usual."

Jane tossed a pillow at Sophie and crawled out of bed. "Time's a wasting, peeps. Let's go."

"Pack your bags," Vicki said, "because once you leave the ship, we won't be coming back until we embark again."

"Yes, Mo-ther," Sophie groaned. She grabbed her bathing suit and towels and stuffed them into a backpack.

"I've got the passports," Tom said. "Let's roll."

The Fryes waited in the line forming to get off the ship. The tourists chattered, lathering on sunscreen and checking for passports as the purser handed out vouchers. Cruise hands bustled, smiling and answering questions.

"Good morning, Mr. and Mrs. Frye," random waitstaff called out.

How can they remember every guest on this cruise ship? He hadn't yet grasped the concept that he and his family were celebrities on the Oceanos.

"Tom-O!" It was JJ.

Tom forced himself to raise a hand and return the high-five offered by the wacky cruise director. But he didn't trust him. The girls had struck up a friendship it seemed, which Tom found odd. Dangerous predators stalked naïve young women. So, he remained vigilant and kept alert.

"Have fun, girls," JJ said to Jane and Sophie. He winked and smiled. "Remember what I told you?" JJ pointed his flag in their direction and tapped Sophie on the head. The girls giggled and smiled, nodding.

"What's that supposed to mean?" Tom asked.

"Chill, Padre," Jane said. "We're strictly in the friend zone."

"Yeah, he's hilarious," Sophie added.

"Well, I think he might be a little old for you, honey," Vicky said.

"Mo-ther, he's like the closest person to our age on the ship. Plus, we totally screened him via social media. He's legit," Sophie said.

"Ah, so you figured out we have unlimited wi-fi?"

"Yes, Dad. JJ enlightened us," Sophie said.

Tom looked annoyed. *Asshole. I wanted to be the one to tell them.* He tried to assess JJ's age; a few laugh lines showed, but the highlighted, spiky hair contributed to his boyish look. Very physically fit. *Probably from carrying around his stupid golf flag.* Tom figured JJ had dipped into services from Unkie's plastic surgery business to look younger. And, he had to admit, JJ remained polite and respectful whenever their paths crossed. He even shared with the Frye family the best route to get to the beach, at Bocagrande, a fifteen or twenty-minute walk once they got off the ship.

"Stake out a spot early, peeps," JJ said. "This beach will be hopping by 11:00."

As predicted, the beach filled up long before noon. The atmosphere gave off a pleasant vibe. Although it lacked the white sand Tom expected, the palm trees and ocean breeze made up for it. The girls settled on a spot close to their parents, and Tom and Vicky rented a cabana from a beach vendor. Vicky baked in the sun, while Tom opted to lounge in the shade.

Nearby food trucks sold street food and drinks. Best of all, there was no sign of the Stabs anywhere.

After a couple of hours, Tom started to get antsy. "Vicky, do you feel like taking a walk? Look around?"

"Sure, let's go tell the girls. Maybe they want to use the chairs."

Their daughters jumped at the chance to take over the cabana. Jane, already burned from lounging by the ship's pool, looked like a lobster. "No worries, parental units. We'll guard the castle. Be safe! Make good choices."

"Smartass." Tom seldom appreciated Jane's sense of humor.

Tom and Vicky walked around the narrow streets, checking out the coffee shops and vendors selling souvenirs. They bought small bags of toffee, a local specialty.

"We should bring some back for the girls," Vicky said.

"No way," Tom replied. "They could've come along. I'm not a delivery man."

Vicky ignored him and bought two small bags to take back. She put them in her purse.

"This stuff is delish." Tom filled his mouth with the soft, gooey confection.

"My feet hurt. I think we should head back to the beach. It'll be time to get on the ship soon."

Tom nodded, stuffing his cheeks with more toffee. Still, he managed to talk with his mouth full. "Okay, but I'd like to check out the square in the plaza over there," he said, pointing down the street.

"Sure. It's in the right direction, anyway."

The square bustled with activity. Vendors sold trinkets and wonderful smells drifted in the air from the food stands. Tom's gaze fell upon a man wearing a colorful costume and a funny hat. *Looks like a court jester. Check out the bells on his shoes.*

"Vick, what's that guy over there doing? The one in the funny costume? Let's go have a look."

When they got closer, they could see the man dressed as an organ grinder. A heavy-duty strap held the ancient looking contraption. He churned the instrument, strolling and attempting to catch the eyes of passersby. In addition, his sidekick—a tiny monkey on a long leash—approached tourists with a tin cup, begging for tips. The monkey wore a tiny red hat with a gold tassel on top.

"Oh, my gosh. Isn't that adorable?" Vicky said.

"Yeah, pretty clever," Tom answered. He popped more toffee in his mouth and chewed. "Let's get a picture. The girls will get a kick out of it." As they stepped close to the man and his monkey, Tom bent down for a closer look. "Hi, little fella."

The monkey stretched out a tin cup. His owner smiled and nodded to Tom and Vicky. "*Buenos dias, amigos.*"

"*Buenos dias,*" Vicky replied. "Oh Tom, do we have any coins for the monkey? He's so cute. Sir, do you speak English?"

"*Si.* Yes."

"What is your monkey's name?"

"Paco, *señora.*"

Tom rummaged in his pockets for some change for the monkey, putting his bag of toffee on the ground while he searched. The monkey moved closer and Tom tossed the coins into the tip cup.

Jumping up and down, the monkey squealed with pleasure. Vicky and Tom laughed along with the organ grinder. Then, quick as a flash, the monkey grabbed Tom's bag of toffee and ran off, racing wildly in circles.

"Hey, he stole my candy. Give that back!"

Vicky and the organ grinder continued to laugh as Tom chased the monkey and tried to recapture his lost candy.

The monkey chattered, teasing Tom. As soon as Tom got close to catching him, the monkey took off in the other direction.

"Tom, this is hysterical. He's teasing you," Vicky said.

"Can't you control your monkey?" Tom asked.

"Ah, he is a free spirit, *señor*. He does as he pleases."

"Bullshit. He's a thief. I want my candy back."

"Okay, okay. I call him back. Paco. *Vamos*."

The monkey crept closer, obeying his master's commands. Tom bent down to snatch the toffee, but Paco began running circles around Tom, entangling him in the leash.

By this time, Vicky had started filming the escapades on her phone. "Hahaha," she laughed. "I can't wait to post this on Facebook when we get back on board."

"Over my dead body. Get this leash off of me, Vicky."

A crowd gathered, with lots of people laughing and taking photos. Tom's cheeks flamed. "Seriously. Do something with your animal," he yelled at the organ grinder.

Struggling to keep a straight face, the man managed to capture the monkey and unraveled Tom from the leash. He grabbed the bag of toffee from Paco's tiny grasp and handed it back to Tom.

Tom looked inside the brown paper bag. "Are you kidding me? Only two pieces left. Your monkey ate a half-pound of my toffee."

"Yes, he likes it very much. It's his favorite. Sorry about that."

"Come on, Vick. Let's get out of here. And stop filming me. This isn't funny."

The crowd chuckled and continued to put money in Paco's cup as Tom grabbed his wife by the hand and pulled her in the direction of the ship.

"I'm starving," Vicky said. "I should've eaten more for lunch."

"Here." Tom tossed her the depleted bag of toffee. "You might as well finish it off."

CHAPTER 16

Back onboard, Tom survived dinner's first seating despite Vicky telling the entire table about his new friend, Paco the monkey. He pretended to laugh along, but inside he fumed. He hated Vicky making jokes at his expense. She even went as far as posting her video on the ship's Facebook page.

Tom excused himself to get a drink from the bar outside the dining room. Brooding, he plotted a way to get back at Vicky, but he couldn't think of anything. *Just wait until the next time she does something embarrassing. All holds barred, baby. Payback is a bitch.* He knew the reality of this ever happening was slim to none. But he pouted nonetheless and pounded the beers.

When he returned to the table, Vicky threw him a dirty look. "Ah, there you are, Tom. I was telling everyone how our landscaping business adventure got started. How you took the leap from finance to Country Bumpkin."

Tom pulled out his chair and sat, facing quizzical looks from the Stabs and the captain. "What is there to tell, Vick?"

"I disagree, Thomas," Mina said. "One minute you were our financial advisor, and the next you were giving us quotes on our landscaping."

"As I recall, Mina, you were preparing to fire me. As your advisor."

"Well, indeed. After the way you behaved, chasing after those poor birds on your lawnmower, swatting at them with the tennis racket. It was shocking."

"As I remember it, Mina, you showed up at my home unannounced and uninvited. I'd say you stalked me. You wanted to see where I lived. Get a look at my home, my wife, my family." Tom's face flamed as his voice grew louder. "Like I clarified before. Unannounced." He glared at Mina and Dr. Stab. "You barged in when I was mowing my lawn. And being attacked by barn swallows. They were dive bombing me when I tried to mow my grass. That's what you saw. Me defending myself against them."

"Ah, I see. Man versus bird? That's absurd."

Vicky interrupted. "I can attest, Mrs. Stab, Tom is telling the truth. Those birds get defensive whenever we mow. It's terrifying how territorial they are when you get close to their nests."

Jane and Sophie nodded in agreement.

"What does this have to do with anything, anyway Mina?" Tom said. "I earned you a lot of money when I managed your accounts, and now I'm trying to *save* you money on your landscaping. Sounds to me like you got a pretty good deal."

"*Humph*," Dr. Stab made a scoffing noise. "You've gotta admit, Tom. It's an odd transition. Broker to Bumpkin?" He and Mina shared a laugh.

"The odd thing, Sam, is that I'd work with you two again."

"Tom," Vicky said. "You don't mean that." She patted him on the back. "I think we've all been out in the sun too long. And teased Tom too much."

"Indeed," Mina said. "Although from the looks of your hands, Thomas, I'd say working out in the hot sun is a regular occurrence." Mina got up, walked over to Tom's seat and grabbed one of his hands. "I wish you'd considered a manicure before this trip. You look like you've been digging ditches."

Tom stood up from the table. "Digging ditches, yes. Planting trees, weeding, mowing, trimming roses. Whatever it takes to make my business successful, Mina. I've never been afraid of a little hard work. Now, if you'll excuse me, I believe I've had enough of this discussion for one evening."

The table dispersed after the awkward confrontation, and Tom returned to the empty cabin and collapsed on the bed, exhausted. But his mind raced, replaying the day's activities over and over. He tossed and turned for a long time but pretended to be asleep when Vicky came to bed later. She fell asleep long before he finally did.

***

When morning rolled around, he remembered they'd be cruising the Panama Canal that day. This cheered him up. Tom looked forward to seeing the great engineering marvel. The ship offered a brief historical overview, and he planned to check it out after breakfast.

Although he'd learned the basics years ago in high school, he figured the refresher course might enrich the experience. His family declined his invitation to join him for the presentation, so he attended by himself. A decent crowd filled up the small auditorium, but not nearly as many as Tom expected. He saw no one he recognized, except for JJ, who made an obnoxious announcement.

"Okay, everyone. Today's the day we see it! The Panama Canal! Are you excited?"

Vague murmurs flitted through the room, acknowledging JJ's question.

"Come on, peeps. Let's show some enthusiasm. Isn't this the number one reason you came on this trip?" JJ raised his signature flagpole high in the air for effect.

The crowd stared, some stirring uncomfortably in their seats.

"Tell me why you're here, sweetie." JJ tapped a middle-aged woman on the top of her head with his yellow flagpole. "What did you come to see?"

"Umm, the blue water," the woman said.

Frowning, JJ moved on to tap a portly gentleman wearing a loud Hawaiian shirt and bright red swim trunks. "How about you, buddy? Why are you here?"

"The food," the man said. "I mean, the buffet is awesome."

"Yes, it is," JJ agreed.

The crowd chuckled. JJ tossed his flag into the corner of the room.

"Moving on," JJ said. "I'm going to introduce our history buff, our own Captain Cosmo Bligh." The crowd clapped without enthusiasm.

The captain bowed and took the portable microphone from JJ who slipped out the back. "Let's get started right away. The inception for a shortcut access between the Atlantic and Pacific Oceans dates to the sixteenth century. It took over ten years to complete and killed about 5,000 people. Ladies and gentlemen, today we'll be traveling through the three locks of the canal—Gatun, Pedro Miguel and Miaflores... "

Tom struggled to stay awake. He'd not slept well the night before, and the combination of dim lights and the captain's monotone threatened to lull him to sleep. A few times he'd caught himself mid-snore and jolted awake in his seat. An elderly woman next to him got up and moved a few seats down the row. *Go ahead and move, lady. It's not my fault this presentation is boring.*

According to the handout the captain provided, the cost for the average cruise ship to pass through the canal started at $330,000. Many of the cruise ships had been built according to the Panamax specifications; not as tall of some of the bigger cruise ships but they could pass trouble-free through the locks. All that money, for what looked like a tight squeeze and a painstaking, slow process.

The captain told the group that with more lanes under construction, the Panamanian authorities anticipated shorter wait times. Eight to ten hours at a minimum still sounded like a long time to Tom. But at least the view came with cocktails.

Forty-five minutes later the captain wrapped up his slide-show presentation and took a few questions from the crowd. To Tom, the questions rehashed the captain's presentation, so he slipped out of his seat in the back row and looked for his family.

He found them, along with a group of other women on the deck, joining in an aerobics class with JJ leading them. Loud disco music from the '70s boomed through the speakers as the ladies jogged in place and pretended to jump rope and do jumping jacks. JJ barked orders, keeping time with his yellow flag and singing along with Donna Summer.

"Move those feet, ladies," JJ barked. "We all want to eat the crème brûlée tonight for dessert." JJ singled out one of the chubbier ladies in the back row, struggling to keep up. "Come on, Delores," he encouraged. "You can do it, girl."

"Oh, for God's sake," Tom said under his breath as he sneaked past the group, hoping to go unnoticed.

"Tom-O! Come join us. Keep me company, bro. I could use another man in the line-up." JJ jogged after Tom. He grabbed his hand, trying to persuade him to join the class.

"Let go of me, JJ," Tom said. "I'm busy."

"Oh, come on. Don't be a party pooper." JJ's stiff moussed hair barely moved in the ocean breeze.

Tom wrenched his hand free and waved the handouts from the captain's presentation in the air as he hurried off. "Gotta run. Lots of historical reading to catch up on." In the distance, he heard Vicky's high-pitched laughter. *Well, here we go again. I'm a laughingstock.*

***

With his family busy elsewhere, Tom walked around the ship. The first day on board, he'd mapped out a walking course for when he needed to be alone. By the time he'd hiked up and down the steps and traversed most of the ship, he'd worked up quite a sweat. As he walked, he thought about some of the interesting things he'd learned.

Tom knew the trip through the locks would move at a snail's pace. The marvel of this whole thing remained the incredibly small amount of clearance the ship had to access. He doubted the zillions of YouTube videos he'd watched could compare to experiencing the real deal. His pulse quickened with anticipation. But he also knew it would test his patience.

After Captain Bligh's presentation disseminated, a large crowd started to gather on the upper decks. For many, traversing the Panama Canal crossed an item off their personal bucket list. The anxious crowd hummed and buzzed, chattering amongst themselves.

"Okay, cruisers," JJ said as he waved his flagpole high in the air. "Today's the day you've been waiting for. We make passage through the three locks of the Panama Canal." He tossed his flag aside and started clapping and swiveling his body back and forth in front of them, encouraging everyone to get fired up. "Without further ado, I'll take any questions you might have before we hurry up and wait."

"So, what will we see today?" a girl asked.

JJ laughed. "Not much!"

Murmurs rippled on deck. Some of the passengers exchanged wary expressions, waiting for further explanation.

"JK, peeps. Just kidding, for those who don't understand kid speak." JJ high-fived the little girl. "Seriously folks, as you can tell, we're in line now... along with a lot of other ships. It'll take a couple of hours for us to pass through the first lock. But it's thrilling. When you see for yourselves that we have only inches to spare on either side of the ship..."

Tom marveled at the long line both in front of and behind the Oceanos.

A tanned, fit twenty-something man raised his hand and shouted, "Hey, JJ. How long does it take to get through all three?"

"Good question, Mike," JJ called back. "A typical trip through the canal for a Panamax cruise ship like ours is eight to ten hours."

Another man closer to the front of the crowd raised his hand. "What *is* there to see?"

"A lot of water," JJ answered. The crowd laughed. "Robert, keep your eyes open and you never know what you might see." JJ smirked. "The scenery is industrial. But remember, folks. This is an engineering marvel. At least the first time you see it. And it's cruisetastic to feel the ship rising with the incoming water as you pass through the locks."

JJ explained how when the ship passed through each successive lock, water released into the narrow space and raised up the ship.

"For me, though, the best part is the end when we're transported magically into the Pacific Ocean." A few people clapped. JJ took a bow and twirled his flag over his head.

"Jesus H. Christ," Tom muttered under his breath. *Where are Vicky and the girls anyway?*

"Any other questions?" JJ scanned the crowd. "Okay, cruisetastic peeps. Enjoy the slow pace of the day and don't forget to tip your bartenders and waitstaff. Right? I'll be roaming around to answer any questions. Enjoy, my darlings."

Disgusted, Tom slipped away from the crowd and decided to return to the cabin to look for his wife and daughters. Today he planned to drink, nap, swim in the pool and soak up the sun. *Why delay?* He looked at his watch. *Nine forty-five. Eh, what the hell? It's five o'clock somewhere, right? But before I imbibe, I need to take care of some business.*

Back at the cabin, his family remained MIA. It didn't matter. Having escaped JJ's shenanigans Tom's mood skyrocketed. So, he changed into his bathing suit and grabbed his iPad. He'd promised Sophie and Jane they'd go ziplining in Costa Rica and he wanted to check for competitive pricing. The ship didn't have an excursion package for any zip tours they could recommend. He needed to find something independently.

Vicky wanted nothing to do with ziplining. *Good. I'm annoyed with her anyway. Hopefully the girls and I can schedule something for the day after tomorrow.*

From time to time, he ventured back up on the main deck to check out the sights, but after watching the ship pass through the first lock, he had to agree with JJ. There wasn't a lot to see.

He tried to remain patient and entertained himself by checking the stock market and browsing through work emails. *Good. Nothing urgent that Walter can't handle.* Bored, he made his way back to the pool to get busy planning the next adventure in Costa Rica. *Screw Vicky if she doesn't want to come along. She can stay on the ship by herself.*

After settling into a comfortable lounge chair, and hailing a server to bring him a drink, Tom surfed the web. He started to get excited by the ziplining pictures in the ads. Tom had fantasized about doing that for a long time, and Costa Rica looked like the ideal spot. Another milestone crossed off his bucket list. He compared a couple of recommendations on Travel Advisor and booked a trio of tickets for Ziplining Adventures, LLC, a company run by an American ex-pat.

The brochure promised triple-cabled secured safety, guaranteed wildlife sightings in their natural habitats, expert guides, transport to and from the ship's port and snacks and tropical drink refreshments. Perfect. He arranged for the company van to pick them up after docking at 10:00 A.M. He couldn't wait to tell the girls.

CHAPTER 17

The next day at sea passed without incident, but tension pulsed through the family. Tom and Vicky interacted when necessary but remained frosty. With so much discord in the air, the girls distanced themselves from both parents and kept a low profile. Vicky pretended to read whenever Tom appeared. He avoided talking to her by scrolling through his tablet, checking on things at the Bumpkin and perusing the stock markets.

When the time came to dress for dinner, Vicky finally bailed and apologized. "Honey, I'm sorry if I upset you. I don't want to fight." She wrapped her arms around Tom.

He returned the hug and stuck his face in her long hair. "Me too. Let's not let it ruin another night?"

"Whew," Vicky pretended to wipe her brow in relief. "Deal. Come on, let's finish getting dressed and go grab a drink to celebrate."

"Perfect. Give me ten minutes to shower and shave and I'm ready to go."

The girls, happy to see their parents reconciled, curbed their sarcastic commentary and behaved well. JJ and the Stabs were dining in one of the alternate restaurants, and the Captain excused himself to attend to some business matter with the purser.

"This is nice. Just the four of us," Sophie said. "I was telling Jane earlier, I'm kinda looking forward to having dinner with fewer people." She laughed. "I mean, at school, I'm surrounded by my sorority sisters, and here on the ship there's always somebody around."

"Truth," Jane said. "But I'm gonna miss it. I think when I graduate, I'll look for a study-at-sea program to get my doctorate." She glanced at her parents for approval, putting on her most charming smile. "Whaddaya think, parents?"

"Not on my dime," Tom said. "Find a rich husband to travel the world with."

"Boo, Padre. Not the answer I hoped for."

Tom chuckled and shrugged. "I live to disappoint you, Jane."

"Enough," Vicky said. "Let's go up on the deck and look at the stars. The moon is full tonight."

"You guys go ahead," Sophie said. "We're meeting JJ later. He's teaching a tango class in the ballroom. Should be hilarious."

"Jeez, sorry to be missing that," Tom said. He and Vicky left the girls to go up on deck. The two stared at the stars, enjoying the sound of the water splashing against the ship.

"Perfect night," Vicky said.

"Uh huh, it is." Tom put his arm around his wife and pulled her close in for a kiss. "I know something that could make it even better." He looked at Vicky, raising his eyebrows. "Whatcha think?"

Vicky looked at her watch. "I think we've got a good hour or so before anyone comes back to the suite. Let's go for it."

Giggling, they made their way back to their cabin. Tom put out the 'Do not disturb' sign.

"Like that would stop anyone from coming in?" Vicky laughed.

"Well, there's always a first time," Tom said, locking the door to their bedroom and turning out the lights. It looked like the night would end well after all.

***

The next morning, Tom roused the family and persuaded Vicky she should come along. "It'll be so much fun, Vick. We can't do it without you. You're gonna regret it if you don't. Please? I promise, I researched this company thoroughly."

"I don't know. It looks terrifying."

"Listen, it's owned by an American ex-pat who is dedicated to safety. He's accredited by the PRCA and the ACCT."

"Yeah, okay. Whatever that means."

"Professional Ropes Course Association, and the Association Challenge Course Technology. They use triple-cabled harnesses. These things get inspected every day and—"

"Okay. I give up. I'll do it."

"Great. I'm sure we can get another ticket when we get there. The guy who's picking us up can let us know for sure."

After disembarking, the family kept a lookout for the guide. Tom paced, checking his phone every few seconds. A lot of tourists buzzed around, chattering about their planned excursions. Some of them speculated whether they should chance traveling too far away.

"Daddy, do we need to worry about missing the ship?" Sophie asked.

"No, honey. I'm sure nothing like that could happen. These guides are used to having to get people back on time. They'd be out of business if they stranded tourists."

Tom's phone buzzed. "He's here. Our guide. His name is Carlos."

"Let's get this over with," Vicky said.

"Says he's driving a red jeep. Ah, I see him over there." Tom pointed to a red vehicle parked about halfway down the busy road. A man waved and Tom waved back. "That must be him. Let's go." The family hurried, anxious to start their adventure.

Their driver, Carlos, held a sign reading, WELCOME TOM FRYE!

"Hey, look at that. Nice, right?"

"We'll see," Vicky said.

"*Carlos es muy caliente*," Jane said under her breath.

"*Si*," Sophie said. "Just your type."

"Stop acting like a couple of cats in heat," Tom said as they approached the guide. "Can't you two control yourselves?" He distanced himself and hurried to shake hands with the driver.

"Welcome," Carlos said. "Are you Mr. Frye?"

"I am, and this is my family."

"Ah, beautiful ladies. It's my pleasure." Carlos grinned and winked at the girls and Vicky. "Are you ready for the adventure of a lifetime?"

"You have no idea," Jane said, batting her eyelashes and smiling.

Carlos opened the car doors for everyone, and Tom and Vicky exchanged a look. They climbed in, with the ladies in the back and Tom riding shotgun.

"So, what part of the states are you from?" Carlos asked as he started the engine and smiled at the girls in the rearview mirror.

"Pennsylvania," the family chimed in unison.

Carlos laughed. "I've been to Philadelphia once. Also Pittsburgh. To visit friends. I make a lot of friends." He winked again and Jane leaned forward, grabbing onto the driver's seat.

"Well, then you've seen all the good parts. Almost, anyway."

Tom interrupted the flirting. "So, Carlos. Your English is good. Did you study in the states?"

"No, sir. We learn English from the time we are babies. The tourist trades demand it. If you want to make a living, anyway. Oh, but the boss told me three passengers. Did somebody extra tag along?"

"Yes, my wife. We convinced her to give it a try."

"Excellent. You will not be sorry, Mrs. Frye. It is a fantastic experience. You'll love it."

"That's what everyone keeps telling me." Vicky sounded uncertain.

"Here we are. Your adventure begins." Carlos continued to make eye contact with Jane in the rearview mirror.

"Will you be joining us, Carlos?" Jane said.

"I wouldn't miss it for the world, miss. Tell me your names, beautiful ladies."

"I'm Jane. This is my sister, Sophie. Oh, and our *mother*, Vicky."

"Ah, I would've sworn you were all sisters."

Vicky gave Jane a smug look. "Aren't you the sweetest thing?"

"Barf-o," Tom said.

"Let the games begin," Sophie said, high-fiving Jane. "Oh my gosh. Look at that, Daddy! Parrots. They're so cute. And monkeys! Up there. In the trees." Sophie pointed out a group of monkeys in the thick, lush palm trees.

Vicky and the girls burst out laughing. "Yay. More monkeys," Vicky said.

Carlos looked puzzled. "You like monkeys, Mr. Frye?"

"No, Carlos. Not really. But apparently, they like me."

The group laughed as they walked toward the entrance.

And here we go again.

CHAPTER 18

"**F**ollow me this way please, ladies." Carlos chuckled. "And of course, you too, Mr. Frye."

Everyone laughed except Tom. "Don't forget, I'm the one with the money."

Carlos turned and put his palms together, bowing in apology. "Of course, sir. Forgive me. We are friends, no?"

"No," Tom said. "I mean yeah, sure. Let's get this over with."

A petite, dark-haired lady greeted them in the office and handed each a clipboard with papers attached. "Please. Read and sign." She pointed to a tiny x at the bottom of the top form.

"*Hmm*, disclaimer forms." Vicky frowned. "This is where we sign away all rights to sue if we are dismembered, maimed, killed, blinded or decapitated, right?"

"I don't know," Tom said. "It's in Spanish." He handed the forms back to the young woman. "*No hablo, señorita.*"

"Padre, please," Jane said.

"Let me help," Carlos said, going behind the counter and rummaging through papers. "Ah, here we are. English." He removed the original paperwork and switched it out with the new forms.

After they all signed and received their tickets, Carlos led the group to the first station. The Fryes and some other guests broke into small groups for training, and watched a short video, explaining the safety features and instructions for the zipline ride.

"Pay close attention. Look to the right for the first set of waterfalls when you get past that group of trees." Carlos pointed off in the distance toward a lush, green canopy. "As you pass through the rainforest, you will see many beautiful native plants and animals."

"What about snakes? Will there be any snakes?" Sophie asked. "I hope not. They terrify me."

Carlos reassured, "There may be snakes, miss. But they are more afraid of you than you need to be of them." He smiled at her. "Plus, you will be a moving target."

Several other people asked questions about the safety of the cables. Carlos explained that the lines were inspected daily. "One cable is actually made up of seven smaller cables woven together, and each of those are made up of nineteen even smaller cables."

He paused and looked around the crowd of twenty. "Don't forget, my friends. You will not be going anywhere without your helmet and gloves. And no one gets past me wearing flip flops. You must wear closed-toe shoes. Safety is our priority here." He paused and winked at Jane and Sophie. "Well, only after fun. Right, girls?"

Anxious to move past the instruction phase, Tom moved closer to Carlos. "I gotta tell you, those harnesses look uncomfortable." He gestured to a man already fitted with the equipment. The triangle-shaped harness snugly gripped the man's crotch. "One false move and I'll be saying *adios* to my favorite body parts."

"Not to worry," Carlos said. "It's very safe. And not as uncomfortable as it appears."

"All the same, I'm glad that guy is going first."

Carlos gave Tom a wan smile and nodded. "Okay, line up over here and we'll get you ready to zip." The group buzzed with excitement, ready for the adventure. Carlos divided them into five groups of four persons. "You made a smart decision to visit us today. Here in Punta Renas, you will have views of the Pacific Ocean, the mountains and rainforests. Plus, we have eleven waterfalls. This tour has views of two of them. Very beautiful ride."

"And monkeys," Jane said sniggering.

"Oh, God. I hope I can keep my eyes open. I'm terrified," Vicky said.

Tom put his arm around her and pulled her close. "I'll go before you, and I'll be right there watching you the whole time as you're coming in to stop."

"Okay," Vicky said. "Still, I'm nervous."

"What are you most afraid of, Mrs. Frye?" Carlos asked.

"That I won't be able to stop. Or control how fast I go."

"Remember, we use a passive braking system here at Ziplining Adventures," Carlos said. "Toward the end of the ride, there is a slight upward slope. This will slow down the ride and allow us to grab you and bring you to a complete stop."

"So, I won't have any control?" Vicky looked panicked.

"Mrs. Frye, we have found this to be the safest method for first-time zipliners. For the riders to not have control of the braking system. All you need to do is enjoy the ride. We will take care of everything else."

"Stop worrying, Mom. It's gonna be great." Sophie bounced up and down. "Can I go first, Carlos?"

"Yes, you certainly can," he answered. "Let's get you ready to go."

After everyone had suited up with their harnesses, helmets and gloves, Carlos led the Fryes to the platform. Sophie couldn't wait, bopping with excitement as Carlos tried to attach her harness to the cables.

"Stand still so he can hook you up," Tom said.

"Okay, okay. I'm trying. But I'm so excited!"

Carlos tugged on the cables, ensuring Sophie's harness was secure. "Are you ready to go?"

"Ready!"

Carlos gave the signal and Sophie glided off into the lush skyline. Tom heard her squealing and laughing off in the distance. He smiled and hugged Vicky. "Sophie's dream has come true."

Vicky nodded. "It's all she's talked about since I won this trip. I love to hear her laughing. It's contagious."

"I'm going next, parental units," Jane said.

"Obviously," Tom said. "We're working our way up the family food chain."

"Ha, ha," Jane said. "Very funny."

"Okay, you're up." Carlos hooked Jane's harness to the cable, and with a loud yelp, she jumped off the platform.

"Typical Jane," Tom said. "Always trying to pick up speed."

"Oh, Tom. I'm so nervous. Maybe I shouldn't do this." Vicky tugged at his shirt sleeve, holding it in a death grip. "I feel like I'm gonna be sick."

"Come on, Vick. It's only nerves. I'll be there waiting for you."

"We haven't lost anyone yet, Mrs. Frye," Carlos said. He patted her shoulder reassuringly. "You'll regret it if you don't go."

"Yeah, plus I already paid for you," Tom said.

"Okay. I'll do it." Vicky looked scared but resigned to participate.

"Okay, my coworker on the end platform has radioed me. He's ready for the next rider. Mr. Frye, you ready to go?"

"Yes, sir. Just be gentle with the family jewels, Carlos."

With the harness secured, Tom adjusted his helmet and gloves. He planted a quick kiss on Vicky's cheek and gave a thumbs up. Smiling, he leaned back slightly and pushed off. He whooped as the line carried him away.

Tom's adrenaline surged and his stomach felt like it had leapt into his throat. *This must be what it's like to fly.* The breeze whipped in his face, the tropical air dewy and moist against his skin. A surreal sensation swept over him, awed by the beauty everywhere he looked. *Oh, there's the waterfall Carlos talked about.* He swore he could hear the falls roaring from the power of the blue water.

Parrots, their bright yellow and green feathers ruffling in the breeze, called to him from their tree perches. Another tree housed a group of monkeys, their eyes wide and dark in their tan faces. He flew along on his line, faster than expected, but he saw everything so clearly, as if suspended in time. Immersed in the experience, the roar of the wind and the whirring of the zipline both thrilled and entranced him. *This is amazing. Oh. There's the other waterfall over there.*

Off to his left he saw the ocean, a sparkling turquoise blue. The view of the beach took his breath away with the bright sunshine winking and glittering off the waves. Then, in an instant, the zipline whisked him away from the coast and carried him back into the rainforest. Its lush green majesty smelled of both life and decay. His senses exploded with the sights and sounds all around him.

As he neared the end of the ride, he realized how this adventure had changed him. He hadn't imagined he would be so affected by the experience. He could see the end platform clearly now, with a man waving him in. The girls jumped up and down, excited to see him. Before he knew it, a staffer named Jose unhooked his harness. Party over. The girls giggled.

"Daddy, we got your picture coming in," Sophie said.

"And Jose got pictures of all of us, too." Jane pointed to an overhead camera, mounted high on a post.

"Yes. For sale in gift shop," Jose said.

"Great." Tom looked peeved. "More money spent."

"Oh, Dad," Jane said. "Let's watch for Mom on the camera."

On a small-screen TV mounted near the control panel, they could see Vicky getting ready for her departure.

"She looks terrified," Jane said laughing.

"Yeah, she always crosses herself before she does anything scary," Sophie said.

"Probably the Catholic guilt thing," Jane said.

"Stop." Tom positioned himself close to the rail. "I want to get a picture of her coming in."

"Dad fancies himself quite the photographer," Jane said to Jose. "But he's really not that good." Both Jane and Sophie laughed.

"Sir, I'm not sure that's a good place to stand," Jose warned. "You could get hurt if she comes in too fast."

"But you control the speed, right?" Tom looked irritated. "We told her the ending would be slower."

"Yes, it is slower. Didn't you notice it yourself?"

"I'll be fine. Don't sweat it." Tom held his position at the railing.

"Ooh, she's getting close," Sophie clapped her hands. "I bet she loves it."

"I disagree. Can't you hear her screaming from here?" Jane said. "We'll never hear the end of this."

"Okay, here she comes," Jose said. He grabbed onto the rope and pulled down to slow her speed.

"This is gonna be a great action shot," Tom said. He crouched down, inching a little closer to the ledge. He poised the camera, ready to snap. As Vicky got closer, Tom started snapping one picture after another. He laughed, hearing her yelling. *She's having fun, despite the fuss she's making.*

As Jose pulled her to a stop, Vicky splayed her legs and plowed straight into Tom. His cell phone flew out of his hand and catapulted into the air, disappearing into the jungle below.

"Oh, no! My phone!"

Oblivious and grinning from ear to ear, Vicky yelled, "Wow! That was great." She looked puzzled when the family moved to the railing and peered over the edge. "Hello? What's wrong with everybody?"

The girls looked truly panicked. Finally, Tom seethed, "Jesus, Vick. I dropped my phone. I tried to take a picture, but you slammed into me."

"Oh, no. Honey, do you think we will be able to find it?" Vicky's hand flew to her mouth as Jose unlatched her from the harness.

"Who knows," Tom said. "But if it landed down there in the water, it'll be ruined. This is un-freakin' believable."

"But, lucky for you, you can pick up your pictures from the zipline cam in the gift shop," Jose said. "You'll still have a picture from today." He grinned and nodded his head up and down. "Right?"

Tom glared at Jose. "Yeah. It's my lucky day for sure." He tossed his helmet and gloves into the collection box and stormed off to look for his phone.

CHAPTER 19

An exhaustive search of the grounds surrounding the zipline's platform yielded nothing. Tom's phone had disappeared into the jungle. And no one had turned anything in to the lost and found.

"It could be anywhere," Tom said. "When it hit the ground, it could've bounced in another direction."

"Yeah, brilliant idea to get the camouflage Otterbox case for your new phone, Tom." Vicky had little sympathy. "Every vacation. Every single one. You lose something."

"I haven't lost you yet."

"*Yet* being the operative word." His wife stomped off in a huff.

"Parents, please don't fight." Sophie, looking close to tears, snuggled up. "I'm so sorry, Daddy. I feel like this is all my fault. It was my idea to zipline."

"No honey, it's nobody's fault." Tom hugged her close and kissed the top of her head. "It'll turn up. And if it doesn't, I'll use the insurance plan they suckered me into buying."

"Yeah, but..."

"Soph, it's okay. I can get a phone when we get home. As long as Mom has hers, it'll be fine. Come on. Let's get out of here. We need to get back to the ship." They picked up their souvenir photos and met Carlos at his jeep.

Carlos escorted the Fryes back to the port and promised to contact Vicky if Tom's phone showed up. The pathetic pictures, of poor quality and higher than expected prices, commemorated their adventure, if nothing else. They bid goodbye to Carlos and climbed out.

"We'd better get going, ladies, or we'll miss the boat," Tom said.

"God, don't even say that out loud," Vicky said.

"Yeah, I'd flip the f out," Jane said.

"Everything flips you out, Jane," Tom said.

At a temporary loss for words, Jane flipped him the bird and charged to the front of the line.

"I still can't believe you lost your phone, Tom."

"Neither can I."

"Even more surprising is how calm you are about this."

"Not much I can do. We looked for it. Called AT&T and told them. Carlos promised he'd let us know if anyone turns it in..."

"Yes, but..."

Tom held up his hand. "I'm a changed man."

"*Mmmhmm*. Time will tell."

***

Back on the ship again, on their private balcony, Tom, Vicky and the girls lounged, soaking up the sun. Tom stared out at the water, wondering what he'd do to entertain himself. "Two sea days till we get to El Salvador. That's a long time."

"I looked at the itinerary. The ship's only docked in Acajutla for six hours. Not much there to do." Vicky slathered on more sunscreen and reached over to smear some onto Tom's face. "You're looking a little pink."

"Not everyone has your tanning capacity, Vick."

"Mom, didn't you say we could use our spa coupons if we didn't want to debark?" Sophie said.

"I'm down," Jane said. "That port looked super lame to me. Who ever heard of Acajutla?"

"Good idea. What do you think, Tom?"

"No. After two solid days at sea, I'll be ready to walk on land. I think I'll get off. You ladies enjoy your spa day."

"Daddy, you should be careful," Sophie said. "I read El Salvador has the highest crime rate in Central America. Lots of gangs. Organized crime."

"You're very sweet, honey. But I think I can take care of myself." Tom rose from his lounge chair and planted a kiss on Sophie's cheek.

"Ha! That's funny," Jane said. "Padre roaming around with the gangs and drug lords." Jane stood up, tossing her beach towel on the floor. "Time for my shower, family."

"Always with the sarcasm," Vicky said.

"It's what I do." Jane laughed. "You're welcome."

"Vick, what do you say we pack it in for today? Grab a couple of drinks and get an appetizer?"

"Ooh, can we come?" Sophie said. "Which bar?"

"I think The Conquistador. I love their nachos," Tom said. "And it's not as crowded as the bars near the dining room. Why don't you meet us there when you've finished getting dressed? Vick?"

"Sounds like a plan," his wife said. "Don't be too long, girls, it's only about an hour until dinner service."

"Yeah, yeah," Jane said.

After a few drinks, supreme nachos and some calamari, they made their way to the dining room. Tom took a few deep breaths, resolved to keep calm. Whenever he started worrying about his lost phone, he forced himself to stop and take some deep breaths. He'd managed to avoid the Stabs most of the time. And despite the stress of the first evening, dinners the subsequent nights proved less intense.

This evening, Dr. Stab and Mina positioned themselves on either side of Captain Bligh, determined to monopolize him. "Do tell us about your relative, *The* Captain Bligh," Mina said. Happy to oblige, the captain launched into a tedious recollection of the *Mutiny on the Bounty* tale. True to form, Sam pounded his Bankers Club cocktails and picked at his well-manicured cuticles.

Relieved the Stabs separated the captain from Vicky, Tom found himself more relaxed. He didn't appreciate the sleazy way Bligh stared at his wife. *God, the guy doesn't even bother to hide the fact he's flirting.* Best to keep Vicky far away from Captain Bligh, the smarmy bastard.

After supper, he and Vicky strolled on the deck, hand in hand, relishing the feel of the salty sea spritz on their skin. The moon hung high in the sky and reflected in the ocean. "I have to admit. I'm enjoying myself more than I thought I would."

"Honey, I'm proud of you. No seasickness. No complaining. No worrying about the nursery."

"Yeah, I feel more relaxed than I have in a long time. Despite losing my phone."

"It does make me nervous. You not having a phone. What if there's an emergency and you're by yourself?"

"I'm a big boy. I survived most of my life without a cell phone." He grabbed her in a tight embrace. "Don't forget. I was a Boy Scout."

"Yeah, I know. But still..."

"Come on. Let's go check out the pathetic entertainment. Get some more drinks?"

"Okay. I heard JJ was leading a karaoke club group. Should be good for a few laughs."

Tom rolled his eyes. "JJ. There's something off about the guy."

"He is related to the Stabs. Don't forget that."

They ventured into the nightclub in time to hear JJ belting out *Burning Down the House.* "David Byrne would throw himself overboard if he heard this crap," Tom said.

Vicky giggled. They spotted Jane and Sophie with a group of other young people. "Should we go say hi?"

"Absolutely. Let's embarrass them whenever possible," Tom said.

"Oh, never mind. Let's sit by ourselves."

Spotted by their daughters, they waved and sat at a table for two on the opposite side of the bar. Tom found it hard to keep a straight face at some of the karaoke singers.

After a string of terrible performances, Mina took the cake with her rendition of *Ring My Bell.*

"That may be the worst thing I've ever heard," Vicky said.

Tom laughed too hard to say anything.

JJ took the microphone from his aunt and clapped as she exited the stage.

"Wasn't that fabu?" JJ asked the crowd. "Let's give it up for my Auntie Mina! A real disco queen." He handed the microphone to the next person in line and picked up his yellow flag. He strutted the stage, waving his flag. "Come on! Who's up next after Andre?" The house spotlight searched the crowd, pausing on random spectators. Then, JJ noticed Tom and Vicky.

"This is too much. I gotta get out of here," Tom said. He stood up as the spotlight caught him.

"Oh. My. Goodness," JJ said. "I spy a Frye. A Mr. Tom Frye." He hustled over to Tom and Vicky's table, picking his way through the crowded bar and waving his flag baton like a bandleader. "Come on, Tom-O. You're up after Andre."

"Absolutely not," Tom said. "I don't do karaoke."

"Oh, come on. Be a good sport," JJ persisted.

"No, thanks. We're leaving."

"Can't say no to the JJ, Tom-O."

"I'm saying no, JJ-O."

"Well, you have to do something. What else can you do? Juggle? Sword swallowing?"

"JJ, that's enough," Tom said. His face grew red. "Stop."

"I'm only kidding, Tom-O." JJ patted Tom's arm. "How about a joke, then? Know any good jokes?" JJ held the microphone closer to Tom, egging him on.

Tom remembered a joke he'd made up earlier in the week. One that he told Vicky and the girls as they passed through the dessert bar. *Eh, what the hell.* "Okay, JJ. I've got a joke for you. What's the official cookie of the Oceanos?"

"*Hmmm.* I don't know, Tom-O. What *is* the official cookie of the Oceanos?"

"Chips Ahoy."

JJ and the crowd groaned. A few people laughed out loud. Tom took a bow and waved. He noticed Jane and Sophie sliding down low in their chairs, embarrassed.

"Oh, brother," Vicky said. "That's my cue. I'm going to bed. Are you coming?"

"Yeah, I'll be there shortly." He finished his drink and decided to leave, trying to ignore the snickering from several of the passengers as he left the bar. *That stupid JJ. Why did I let him play me like that? I'll get that little prick back.* So much for his changed attitude.

CHAPTER 20

The blaring loudspeaker in the cabin woke him. "Good morning, cruisers." JJ's grating voice made Tom grit his teeth. "Time to rise and shine if you're planning to debark. We should be docking by 8:00 A.M., so chop-chop."

Tom groaned and rolled over, covering his head with his pillow. "Seriously? This asshole is broadcasting so early. It's 6:30."

Vicky yawned and sat up in bed. "Yeah, but you're the one who's leaving the ship today. Remember?"

"Ugh, don't remind me. I guess I'd better get up. Can we turn that speaker off?"

"Nope. It's not an option. It's there for emergency broadcasting or something. Urgent ship announcements."

Tom dragged himself to the bathroom and turned on the shower. "There's nothing urgent about that weirdo." JJ's blabbing continued to boom over the loudspeaker and pound in Tom's ears. Even with the shower running full-force and the exhaust fan whirring, Tom heard the voice echo in the tiled bathroom.

Every morning, JJ held court over the ship's loudspeaker with his assistant, another lackey on the ship. *I guess this guy is his side kick.* "These two have the worst morning talk show I've ever heard," Tom yelled to Vicky as he toweled off.

"Before I sign off, cruisers, I have a joke for you. What's the official cookie of the Oceanos? Give up? Chips Ahoy. Hahaha! Everyone have a cruisetastic day! JJ is signing off. See you on deck at 9:00 if you want to catch the shuttle to the craft market. *Ciao.*"

Tom threw his towel on the ground and stomped to his suitcase. "That little shit. He stole my joke."

"It's a horrible joke, Tom." Vicky got out of bed and went into the bathroom.

"But it's my joke, Vick. He stole it."

"You better grab some breakfast if you're going into town, Tom." Vicky yawned again. "The girls and I made reservations at the spa for 9:30. We should be finished by the time you get back on board." She finished brushing her teeth and came out to kiss him goodbye. "Please, be careful."

"Yeah, yeah. Bye." Tom threw on his shorts and grabbed his wallet from the bedtable. *What a way to start the day.*

Dozens of cruisers assembled below deck waiting to disembark. JJ pranced up and down the line, checking for passports and excursion tickets.

"Okay, everyone." JJ pounded his pole and blew the whistle around his neck to get the cruisers' attention. "We want to have a cruisetastic time today, so let's cover some ground rules." He moved among the crowd, making eye contact with each of them. "First, remember please we're only disembarked a few hours. Plenty of time for this island. We've scheduled a courtesy shuttle to take us to the craft market."

"What else is there to see here?" a familiar voice asked from the back of the line.

Tom whirred around. *Mina.* She was decked out in a white linen suit, floppy white hat, and carrying a striped white parasol. *Oh, God. Please. No.*

"The craft market is super cute, Auntie," JJ said. "Great place to hunt for souvenirs. Books about the Mayan ruins, artifacts. Also, a café where you can get coffee—lots of coffee plantations in El Salvador. There's a small park that the tourist board put together. Nice place to relax and people watch. Benches. Food trucks so you can grab a snack."

The ship eventually cleared immigration and the group left the ship.

"Oh, look. There's the shuttle bus." JJ chatted with the driver as he waved passengers onto the bus, a rundown jalopy with all its windows wide open.

Anxious to walk on land after a couple of days at sea, Tom wasted no time staking out a seat in the front of the bus. *The faster I get off this thing the better. But how can the driver see out of that windshield? It's so caked with dead bugs and dirt. No air-conditioning in this neck of the woods, I guess.* With the windows down, and red dust flying up from the tires and into the bus, they drove to the craft market.

"Is it safe?" one of the cruisers asked JJ.

"Stick to the designated areas and you'll be fine." JJ took a sip from his water bottle. "But there are criminals here that prey on tourists—same as any tourist hot spot. So be careful. Ladies, use those crossbody straps on your purses. Guys, please use front pockets for your cells and wallets. Any other questions?"

He scanned the group, raising an eyebrow. "Okay, we've arrived, darlings. It's 9:30 A.M. I need everyone assembled at the craft market entrance at twelve o'clock sharp. Do not be late!"

"Hey, JJ. We're on our own for food, right?" Tom asked.

"Yes. Lots of fun local stuff to try." JJ did a quick head count before setting them free. "And the coffee is to die for, Tom-O." He ran his hand through his spikey hair. "Okay, peeps, remember. One o'clock. And don't let any taxi drivers or hucksters talk you into a tour of the Mayan ruins. They're four hours away. You'd never make it back in time."

In many ways, Acajutla looked like any other port of call. Palm trees waving in the sea breeze, tourists milling about in over-sized hats and sunglasses, burning to a crisp. Tiny huts and outbuildings with peddlers and food trucks dotted the perimeter of the craft market. To entice the tourists' taste buds, merchants sold native fruits along with a variety of local street food and drink concoctions. Tom's stomach growled as the mouthwatering smells filled the air. *I should've listened to Vicky and had breakfast.* He perused the stands. Some of the vendors offered samples. It all looked delicious.

Trying to decipher the menu proved difficult, so he hung out at the stands and observed the cooks. Something called *pupusas* looked and smelled delicious. The chef stuffed thick corn tortillas with meat, cheese and vegetables and fried them until crispy brown. Tom held up a finger to the vendor. He couldn't resist trying one.

But he also bought some empanadas, which looked much like the ones he'd had in the states—delicious flour pastries filled with meat, potatoes and cheese. To round out his sampler platter, he finished with two tamales—boiled pockets of corn dough stuffed with meat, sweet corn and served in steamed banana leaves. He groaned with pleasure.

Sitting on a bench outside the market, he washed it all down with a local beer. And then chased it down with two more. *Well, that was amazing.* Not to mention cheap. He belched and stood up to stretch, ready to explore.

The craft market had a rustic charm. Tom enjoyed walking around and checking out the souvenirs and local crafts for sale. Ramshackle tiki huts served as an outdoor bazaar for the peddlers. As in many other ports on this cruise, poverty loomed large next to the spendthrift tourists. Dirty children ran unsupervised in the dusty marketplace, barefoot and clothed in rags. Weary parents did little to intervene. Begging was commonplace; the police appeared indifferent. Tom spotted several armed men patrolling the area. *I guess they're cops. But they look pretty sketchy to be the police.*

One of the tiki hut inhabitants came around to the front of his shack and smiled at Tom. He waved him over, pointing to his displays and trinkets for sale. "American?" he asked in halted English. "You buy?" He held up several pieces of jewelry. Silver stuff, Tom imagined, studded with pretty rocks and stones.

Tom shook his head. "No, thanks. Not today."

The man grabbed Tom by the sleeve. "Look. See. Look." He pointed and pulled Tom closer to his stand.

"Okay, I'll look." Tom moved past the jewelry to a display of rustic pieces, little statues that looked hand-carved. And old. Tom picked up a small idol and turned it over in his hands. The statue reminded him of a troll doll he'd had as a kid. Except this wasn't a mass-produced plastic toy. This looked legit. In fact, he suspected it might be an authentic, ancient Mayan relic. *Very cool. This would look fantastic on my desk in the office.*

"You like? Mayan," the man said. "You like? Five dollars. Good deal."

"I don't know."

"You like. Buy?"

"Where did this come from? Is it real?"

"Yes. Real. Mayan. Idol. You buy? Four dollars."

Intrigued, Tom couldn't resist. "Yeah, okay. Four dollars." He pulled the money out and handed it over. *It's probably fake, but I like it anyway.* Tom seldom bought trinkets when he traveled, but he wanted this statue. *Wait till I show Vick and the girls. They'll be sorry they didn't come along with me.*

Waving goodbye, Tom turned around and stopped in his tracks. *Oh, for the love of God. Of all people.* Mina stepped in front of him and blocked his path.

"What's that you've got there, Thomas? May I see it?"

"Just a little something I picked out." He held the statue up tentatively and brought it down again, putting it behind his back.

"For heaven's sake, don't hide it. I didn't get a good look."

Seeing no escape, he held it out for her to examine.

"Hmm, well isn't that darling? I want it."

"What? You can't have it. It's mine."

"You can pick something else out, can't you? You owe me a favor. After all, I agreed to use your floundering landscaping company, didn't I? You should give me the statue as a present. It's charming. Very rustic. I love it."

"Too bad. Find your own souvenirs." Tom's nostrils flared. "And my company is not floundering."

"Give it to me. Now." Mina's voice rose in pitch and volume.

"No, Mina. He's got lots of other stuff over there." Tom pointed to the man's stand, his voice loud and angry. "I'm sure you can find something else. Now buzz off."

"I beg your pardon. You don't say no to me, Thomas." Mina reached over and yanked the idol out of Tom's hands and tried to walk off.

Tom chased after her, grabbing the statue back.

Screaming, Mina hit him over the head with her parasol and tried to get custody of the idol. But Tom held fast.

She continued to beat him over the head, with Tom hanging onto his prized object. After a particularly violent whack, Tom had had enough. He pushed Mina down onto the dirt road. "Stop!" he screamed.

"Help! Help! I've been assaulted," Mina yelled as she tried to stand up. "Someone, call the police!"

The little man who owned the hut began waving his arms and yelling. "*Policia! Vamos!*" The man blew through a horn. It sounded primitive, but effective. And loud.

That's when Tom saw four armed, uniformed men moving rapidly toward the vendor's stand. Machine guns drawn, running straight for them. *Oh. Shit.*

CHAPTER 21

He felt the sharp end of a machine gun jabbing him in the back. The man nudged Tom between his shoulder blades, yelling in Spanish. Message received. Tom stood slowly.

"*Americano?*" the soldier asked.

"Yes. *S-s-si, señor,*" Tom stammered.

One of the other guards yanked Mina from the ground and shoved her next to Tom. "This is unacceptable!" she said. "I've never been so mistreated in my whole life. Are you the police?"

"*Silencio.*" A huge, burly man with wild curly black hair and a bushy moustache growled at Mina and Tom. Towering over everyone, his mere presence commanded respect and instilled fear. He barked instructions to the other three guards.

They all responded, "*Si, General.*"

He must be the head honcho. The General. Tom's legs quivered and he thought he might pass out. *Oh, God. Not now. Not a panic attack.* He hadn't had one in months. *Stay calm. Think.*

"Are you the police?" Mina repeated. "I wish to file a complaint against this man."

"*Silencio!*" the general said again. He looked back and forth between Mina and Tom, then focused his attention on Tom. "You. Your wife? This woman?"

Tom stifled a nervous laugh. "Oh God, no."

Mina scoffed. "Honestly, I never..."

"Hush," Tom said through gritted teeth. "Please."

"You speak English, sir? I mean, General?" Tom asked.

"Yes."

"Oh, good. You see our ship is only here for six hours, and we need to get going, so…" Tom looked at his watch. "We need to get on the shuttle back to the ship at noon."

"You're not leaving, *señor*. Not yet."

"What? I mean, why not?"

"Stealing is a serious crime, *señor*."

"Stealing? I haven't stolen anything. Ask that guy. The one in the stand." Tom gestured, pointing to the tiki hut where he had purchased the idol. But when he turned around, the man had disappeared. In fact, all the shops looked as if they had closed for the day, with the shutters closed and locked up tight.

"Do you have proof? A receipt?"

"No. I paid cash. Four dollars."

"Four dollars?" The general laughed. "For that? That is criminal. That is a relic. Valuable. From the Mayan empire."

"What?" Tom said. "The guy sold it to me. He named the price. I bought it." He turned and pointed at Mina. "And then *she* tried to steal it from me."

The general barked quick orders in Spanish to his crew, and in an instant, they slapped handcuffs on Tom and Mina.

"Hey! What's going on?" Tom said. "Ow. You can't do this."

"Help! Help! Police!" Mina screamed and thrashed between two of the men.

The general laughed. "*Señora*, we *are* the police." All the men laughed along with him. "Cooperate and there will be no problem."

"Look, this is a huge misunderstanding," Tom said. "I can explain. If we can find the guy that sold this to me…"

"Siesta time, *señor*. Shops are closed until later tonight."

With their guns drawn, the general and his men forced Tom and Mina toward a large SUV parked outside the market. During the short walk, Tom searched for any sign of JJ or the shuttle bus. But, to no avail. No sign of anyone from the cruise was in sight.

Tom's mind raced. He had managed to end up in police custody in a third world country, where he didn't speak the language. Without his cell, he had no way to communicate with his wife and let her know what had happened. He struggled to take deep breaths and stay calm. *Oh my God. The ship is gonna leave without us.*

He looked at Mina as the police shoved her in the vehicle. She thrashed around, yelling for help. One of the men took out a dirty red bandana and gagged her. She kept trying to yell, but her muffled screams went unnoticed by the few locals still outside. Most people had headed home for their afternoon siesta, and anyone who might have heard, looked away, not wanting to implicate themselves. They loaded Tom into the vehicle next.

With both Tom and Mina confined in the backseat, the driver peeled out of the parking lot. In his head, Tom replayed Sophie's warnings to him, telling him about the high crime rate and the corrupt government. A lump in the back of his throat made it hard to swallow. He contemplated the real possibility he may never see his family again. A small sob escaped him, but he cleared his throat and tried to regain his composure. He tried to ignore the smug expressions on the faces of the police.

"Where are you taking us?"

"Police headquarters," the general laughed. The other men laughed and said something in Spanish. They all nodded, and the driver accelerated.

It feels like we've been driving a long time. We're headed away from civilization. And this looks so isolated.

Tom glanced at his watch, but the handcuffs blocked his view. He guessed it had to be past noon. They'd missed the ship. He knew that much.

The SUV bounced along the dusty dirt roads. No sign of civilization anywhere, they headed deeper into the jungle. Without seatbelts, Tom and Mina jostled under the watchful eyes of their captors. *No shock absorbers in this thing. This has international incident written all over it. How could I be so stupid? I should've never gotten off the ship. Holy shit. This cannot be happening. With Mina, of all people.*

Well into the dark jungle, the sunlight slipped in tiny glints through the windows. The lack of light increased Tom's terror and fueled an urgent need to use a restroom. Pronto.

"I need a bathroom," Tom said.

"You'll have to wait. Hold it," the general said and smirked.

"It's an emergency."

"We are almost there. You can go then."

Yeah, I hope so. For everyone's sake. He shuddered at the thought of losing control of his bowels. *Keep it together, Tom.*

The SUV slowed, making the ride even more agonizing for Tom. He struggled to keep breathing deeply and willed himself to stay in control. After they jostled along for a few more minutes, they arrived at what looked like a military compound. Two flags billowed high in the steamy air. *The flag of El Salvador, maybe? But what's the other one?* A guard stepped out of a ramshackle hut and waved the SUV through. Clearly, they knew the general's car and his driver.

A short dirt road led to a camp scattered with primitive buildings and faded canvas tents. *Military surplus? What is this place?* Tom looked around and wondered who had abducted them. *This was no police station. Some kind of guerilla operation, maybe? Drug lords? Military?* He wished now that he'd paid more attention to the covert operations in Central America. *Shit.*

When the SUV stopped, guards forced Tom and Mina from the vehicle. Mina's eyes opened wide with terror. Still gagged, she appeared resigned to cooperating with their captors.

"Uncuff him," the general barked to one of his subordinates, "and show him the latrine."

Before unlocking the handcuffs, the man asked the general something in Spanish. The general nodded his consent and the guard unlocked the cuffs. The guard held tight to Tom's forearm and steered him past numerous outbuildings until they came to the latrine.

"I watch you," the guard said, pointing his gun at Tom. "You go in." The guard threw open the door to the outhouse. Tom heard flies buzzing even before he got inside. The smell was so foul, he gagged.

Humiliated, Tom dropped his pants and crouched over the crude opening. He'd never had to take a shit with someone watching him, but he had to go. He'd barely lasted through the car ride. *I've hit a new low. Kidnapped and forced to defecate under surveillance.*

Smirking, the guard lit a cigarette and kept watch. "You hurry."

"Believe me, I will," Tom said under his breath, relieved to see the roll of scratchy toilet paper in the stall. *Thank God.*

Mission accomplished, Tom walked out of the outhouse and looked around.

"What?" the guard said. "What now?"

"Can I wash my hands?"

CHAPTER 22

A female soldier escorted Mina to the latrine while another guard ushered Tom into an interrogation room. They confiscated his wallet and took his watch and wedding ring.

Tom found the general siting at a long table with a couple of folding chairs on either side. As instructed, Tom sat opposite him. A few armed soldiers stood guard. To his surprise, they offered him a bottle of water and he accepted it with gratitude. All the salty food he'd eaten earlier, coupled with his anxiety, had left him parched.

The general kept mum. He stared at Tom with a blank expression. Dark and windowless, the room had no breeze circulating whatsoever. The musky smell of body odor permeated the air, and Tom couldn't get the awful smell of the latrine out of his nose. *How could this be happening? I should be on the ship, breathing fresh air on the deck with my wife. Oh, God. Poor Vicky. She must be out of her mind wondering where I am.* Fearing he might vomit, Tom sipped the water slowly, and tried taking deep breaths, no matter how foul the conditions.

He heard Mina coming before he saw her. She sounded furious. He sighed and started a silent prayer. *Please, God. Help us out of this mess. I'm not sure what's happening, but I've never been so afraid in my life. Please, Lord. My family needs me. Please. Help us get out of here.*

After the kidnapping and her trip to the outhouse Mina looked pathetic. If he'd found himself in different circumstances, he might get a kick out of her disheveled appearance. Her white clothes, splotched with dirt and ripped in the struggle, spoke volumes. Few traces remained of the woman who'd shown up earlier in impeccable makeup with expertly coiffed hair.

Despite his anger, for a split-second Tom pitied her, knowing how appalling she'd find herself in a mirror. Then he remembered why they found themselves in this predicament and got angry again. He found the courage to speak up. "So, what's going on here? Why're you holding us?"

"Clearly, you are not the police," Mina said. "I have dual citizenship. I demand immediate contact with the United States Embassy and the Swedish Embassy."

Tom groaned and ran his hand through his hair. "Mina. Calm down."

"You need to be quiet, woman," the general said.

"I beg your pardon. You have no right—"

"Get the gag again," the general interrupted. "If you can't shut your mouth, I will do it for you. Put her back in handcuffs."

Mina stood and screamed, "I demand you release me." Two guards held her as the female soldier replaced the gag and put the handcuffs on again.

"I will talk to *you*, Mr. Frye," the general said. "Since the woman does not wish to cooperate." He looked at the driver's license in Tom's wallet and checked the billfold. "You don't carry much cash, do you? And only one credit card?"

"Never carry more than I can afford to lose," Tom said. "Is this about money? Is that what you are? Kidnappers?"

Laughing, the general leaned back in his chair. He pulled a cigar out of his pocket and ran it under his nose before lighting the tip with a match. "Kidnapper is such an ugly word, Mr. Frye." He puffed his cigar and blew a stream of smoke toward the ceiling.

"What would you call it then?"

"Venture capitalists, I think."

"Well, you see I haven't got any money. I don't even have a phone. Why not let us go?"

"No. Not yet anyway." He continued puffing and blew smoke rings. "Besides, I think she is the one who is rich, no?" He pointed to Mina, restrained and sullen in her chair. He hauled Mina's designer bag from the floor to the table and dumped the contents. The general focused on the leopard-print wallet stuffed with cash. He splayed a thick stack of hundred-dollar bills and fanned himself, still puffing on his fat cigar.

Tom stared at the motherload of expensive paraphernalia spilled from the Prada bag. Designer cosmetics, Ray-Ban sunglasses, iPhone, and a gem-encrusted leather passport case.

"You see? All the things she carries. On an island like this." The general laughed. "Not to mention her jewelry. What else must she have?"

Tom said nothing but turned his hands over and picked at a callous on his palm. *I need a plan. But what?*

The general raised an eyebrow and laid the cash aside. He grabbed Tom's hand and examined it closely. "You, Mr. Frye, do not look like you have much money." He turned Tom's hands over and then released them. "Yours are the hands of a man who works hard. A laborer. No?"

At first, Tom got angry. *This asshole has no idea how much money I have. If only he knew what I was worth.* But he kept his face blank and kept quiet. *Pride will not serve you well, Tom-O. Boy, I'd give anything to see JJ's face in the doorway right about now. He must be freaking out, too. Auntie is missing. But that might work to our advantage.*

Tom and the general continued to stare at one another and said nothing. Eventually, the general broke the silence. "I speak the truth, don't I? You have nothing. How did you afford to go on this cruise?"

"My wife won a trip."

"Ah. That explains it!" The general chuckled. "No spending money for you, eh? You had to buy yourself a cheap souvenir? The little idol."

"Yeah, that didn't turn out so well," Tom said.

"Ah, maybe if you behave, I'll give it back to you. Eh?"

Tom minded his tongue and kept silent. *Okay, don't do or say anything rash. There's gotta be a way out of this. Think.*

The general smoked his cigar and rearranged Mina's cash into neat stacks. "I cannot get blood from a stone, so to speak," the general said. "You are not much use to me, I think." He pointed to Mina and smirked. "But that one. She is a different story."

Mina squirmed, eyes wild and furious. She grunted and thrashed in her chair. The female guard pointed the end of her gun against Mina's head.

The general spoke to Tom. "Tell her to stop moving," He pointed to Mina. "You know her. Yes?"

"Yes."

"From before the trip?"

"Yes."

"How?"

Mina thrashed in her chair, straining against the handcuffs. The guard struck her with the gun and Mina's head dropped to one side. Tom struggled to quiet the scream in the back of his throat. *Keep calm. Deep breaths, Tom.*

"I worked at her home. As a landscaper."

The general looked puzzled. "What?"

He doesn't understand the word. Think. "Um, a gardener. Took care of her grass, plants."

The general nodded in understanding.

"She is wealthy. Yes?"

Tom looked at Mina, nodding in and out of consciousness. "Yes."

"How? How does she make her money?"

"Her husband is a doctor. A surgeon."

Rubbing his hands together, the general laughed. "Ah, I knew it. Rich bitch. Very good." He stood hiking up his pants and put his thumbs through his beltloops. "Yes. This is good." He rattled off rapid instructions to the guards. One of them picked up Mina, tossing her over his shoulder. They left the building.

The general tossed Tom's wallet to him, but he examined the watch and wedding ring. "I will give you your wedding ring back, I think," he said. "But I like the watch. I will keep that for myself." He strapped it on his wrist and smiled. "Yes, very nice watch."

"My wife gave that to me for Christmas," Tom said trying to keep the anger out of his voice.

"Well, I do not think she will mind if she gets you back without it, *amigo*. No?" The general snickered. "Did she win that as a prize, too?"

"Yes," Tom lied. "As a matter of fact, she did."

"Ah, well. Here." The general pulled the idol out of a duffle bag and handed it to Tom. "Take your idol. That's a fair exchange. No?"

"You're letting us go?" Tom's voice quivered.

"I'm letting *you* go."

"What about Mina?"

"No, I think I will keep her for a time. But she is a difficult woman." The general rolled his eyes and put his cigar out on the dirt floor. "I hope we don't have to kill her before we can get some money from her husband."

Tom blinked. "What? What do you mean? You're not letting her go?"

"Not yet. But that should not concern you. I will have one of the men take you close to the edge of town. Drop you off. You should be able to find your way to the port." The general raised his hand and snapped his fingers. One of the guards came up behind Tom and tied a blindfold around his head, covering his eyes.

"Please," Tom said. "What's happening? You aren't going to shoot me, are you?"

"I told you, Mr. Frye, we are returning you. But we must blindfold you."

"Where's Mina? I'm sure her husband will pay your ransom."

"No doubt," the general said. "*Adios,* Mr. Frye. Take him back."

The guard pulled Tom from the chair and pushed him forward. "Move."

"Come on. I can't leave her here."

"*Vamos,*" the guard said. "Walk."

But Tom struggled against him. "General. Please. Let us both go. I can't just leave her here alone."

The general barked orders to the guards and they untied the blindfold.

"Very well, Mr. Frye. Suit yourself." The general pushed Tom back into his seat. "You want to protect her? Play hero? Fine. You can both stay."

CHAPTER 23

After a terrifying night in the dark prison, Tom and Mina found themselves in dire conditions the following morning. Although their concrete, windowless jail cells protected them from the tropical downpours, it didn't keep out the rats or cockroaches. In the dim light, Tom watched Mina from across the room in his cell. He suspected she had suffered a concussion after the guard struck her with the gun. Most of the time, she sat in a stupor and communicated only when necessary—to use the restroom or ask for water.

By the second day in captivity, Tom started recognizing the guards, who appeared to work in short shifts, including several women. He wondered if they had any choice in their line of labor or if they'd been inducted by boyfriends or husbands who forced them. Tom suspected the guards dabbled in drug smuggling and represented local gangs.

The kidnappers kept them fed and hydrated, and every couple of hours, one of the guards would uncuff them for a bathroom break and a chance to stretch their legs. *Considering the circumstances, things could be a lot worse. Probably determined to keep us alive until they can get ransom money.*

Out of fear, Tom treated them with respect, smiling and offering gratitude whenever they granted some small kindness.

"Thank you," he said when a heavily pregnant woman brought him some water and a plate of stringy meat and rice.

She offered a shy smile and nodded.

"When is your baby due?" Tom pantomimed a pregnant belly and rocking a baby.

The young woman stopped to consider the question. She responded with two fingers, and then crossed herself.

"Two weeks?"

She nodded and patted her round stomach. Then she reached around and grasped her lower back and indicated she'd had her fill of this pregnancy. Tom remembered how Vicky suffered at the end of her two pregnancies. He pitied the poor girl. "Soon," he said and smiled at her.

The conversation caught Mina's attention and she perked up. "Why are you talking to those animals?" she called. "You're wasting your time. They're going to kill us."

"Mina, be optimistic. We're not dead yet."

Mina scoffed. "No. Not yet. But I don't understand why you didn't leave when you had the chance. I certainly would have."

Tom wondered how Mina knew he'd had the chance to leave but opted to stay. *The general must have told her.* "I don't doubt that for a minute, Mina."

Each day, the guards escorted them to meet one-on-one with the general. He yelled and screamed, prodding Tom with questions, most regarding how much money the Stabs had and whether he thought Dr. Stab would pay a ransom.

Tom reiterated the obvious. "Yes. They have lots of money. Some properties. And cash, I guess. Dr. Stab will pay to get his wife back."

"I will make my first contact with the doctor in the next day or so." The general folded his hands and stared into Tom's eyes. "A few days with no word will serve us well. By now they are starting to panic." He laughed, tormenting his prisoner. "You must be sorry now, too. That you chose to stay here and defend her honor. Fool."

"Are we done?" Tom said and rose from his chair.

"We're done when I say so," the general said and pounded his fist on the desk. "You know more than you are telling me,

Frye. I can tell when someone is lying. Don't make me punish you for protecting the woman."

Tom said nothing but gritted his teeth. Every day his anxiety mounted. He couldn't last much longer in this hell hole. And Mina was a mess. No help at all. He needed to find a way out of this. But now the general suspected he withheld information. *What does he think? He couldn't know I was their financial advisor, could he?*

"I told you everything I know," Tom repeated. "The house is big. I worked there, planting flowers, mowing grass. I was supposed to put in a fountain soon. But now, well..."

He'd withheld the fact JJ worked for the cruise line, holding onto the hope a rescue might be underway. God knows what transpired in the meetings between Mina and the general. He feared the worst.

Tom doubted the cruise line would involve itself in international kidnappings. But they must have reported Tom and Mina's failure to return to the shuttle bound for the Oceanos. Tom assumed the ship had sailed as scheduled. *Cruise ships wait for no one.*

The general looked skeptical. "*Pfft.* Fountain? If you know what's good for you, you'll tell me everything. Anything that could make a difference. I plan on asking a huge ransom for that woman." He stood up from his desk and waved Tom out of his chair. "Go. I'm finished with you. For now." He hailed the guard over. "Take him."

Handcuffed again, and with a gun pointed at his back, Tom's legs wobbled on the walk to the jail.

***

When he returned to his cell, Mina threw him a scathing look. "Back so soon from your private party, Thomas?"

"What's your issue, Mina? All I've tried to do is get us out of here."

"Ha, that's a laugh. What have you done? Except make that lunatic general think he can squeeze a fortune out of me. It will never happen. Sam is probably working on my rescue as we speak."

"Mina, I haven't told him anything he hadn't already figured out."

"Indeed. He told me. You spilled the beans. Told him we had a fortune."

"That's a lie. I told him I was your landscaper. Your gardener. That I mowed your grass, for Christ's sakes."

"I don't believe you."

"Maybe I should ask you, Mina. What did you tell him? Did you tell him I was your financial advisor?"

They stopped speaking when a guard burst through the door. "What is going on here?" He looked back and forth between Tom and Mina and shook his fist. "Be quiet. No more shouting. The general does not want any trouble. *Silencio*."

Tom closed his eyes and tried to nap. The bed, an old military cot, had no support, but it beat sleeping on the floor.

After a couple of hours, the guards took them outside for exercise. Tom scanned the area, trying to observe as many details around him as possible. Ramshackle huts and tar paper buildings dotted the camp, and it appeared a lot of the equipment had been requisitioned from military surplus. Several old jeeps and motorcycles scattered the perimeter of the camp.

The residents, many marked with tattoos, exuded an angry aura, casting scathing looks at the prisoners. *They must be members of a gang, or a drug cartel.* They loaded and unloaded unmarked boxes into vehicles. Then, quick as lightning, they drove off in a cloud of dust. The area buzzed like a beehive.

Tom noticed animals in the vicinity of the camp as well. A bunch of goats ran unsupervised through the grounds and numerous donkeys grazed in the nearby field. He also spotted a few chickens, and a pathetic attempt to grow crops in a dusty garden plot. The tops of corn tassels waved in the hot breeze, along with some other plants he couldn't identify from this far away. *There must be a well over there somewhere. For the animals and the crops.*

When they returned to their cells after exercise time, the young pregnant girl delivered their evening meal. He smiled and took the food from the woman. *God, she must be miserable in this heat.*

Leaning over to shovel a mouthful of his dinner, Tom caught wind of his armpits and grimaced. After multiple days without a shower, he smelled ripe. At least eating dinner would help pass the time. No matter how awful the food. He tried not to imagine what sort of protein they'd speckled through the concoction. *But dear God, I would kill for something to read. Anything to divert my paranoid imagination.*

Mina tossed her plate of food aside, dumping its contents onto the dirt floor. "I can't endure this slop any longer. Yesterday I found a worm in my gruel."

"Extra protein. But Mina, don't spite yourself into starvation. You need to eat."

She said nothing but turned her back away from him.

Tom continued to eat, until a scream pierced the air. Both Tom and Mina jumped up. The young woman had doubled over, crying out in Spanish. Within a minute or two, several guards ran in, guns drawn.

"*Que es esto?*" one of them asked the girl, who continued to scream.

A flurry of questions erupted as they led the woman to a chair in the corner of the jail. Tom and Mina tried to eavesdrop, but the language barrier interfered.

A few moments passed, with the guards speaking quietly to the woman. The guards pulled her to her feet, and she leaned heavily on them as they steered her toward the exit. That's when the woman groaned and stopped. She bent over, her pants and shoes suddenly drenched in a flood of liquid.

"Oh my God," Tom gasped. "I think her water just broke."

CHAPTER 24

"Waaah!" The woman's wail, entrenched in pain, echoed through the concrete walls of the jail. Her cries sounded so pathetic and wild, the hair on the back of Tom's neck stood on end.

He observed one of the guards bringing a chair for the pregnant lady, and she struggled to sit. After her water broke, a flurry of activity erupted in the jail. Guards barked orders and within minutes, several other female residents of the camp rushed in. They fawned over her and talked amongst themselves. The patient cried out. No one in the jail appeared to know what to do.

Although Tom watched and listened from his cell, the language barrier made it difficult. *These women must be used to home births. This can't be uncommon. Can it? Something else is going on. But what? And what's up with Mina? She looks way too interested.*

"Bring back happy memories, Mina?"

"I beg your pardon."

"Memories. Of the births of your children."

"Absolutely not. I would never consider giving birth in an unsterile environment. How vile."

"Oh, right," Tom said. "Being the wife of a doctor and all. And a nurse."

Mina scoffed. "This is barbaric."

"Ahh! Ahhhhh!" The woman kept screaming.

"She needs a doctor," Tom said.

"Oh, yes. I'm sure she has her pick of all the best obstetricians in the camp." Mina walked to her cot and sat on its edge.

The general burst through the door and ran to the pregnant woman. "Lupe?"

He brushed back her long hair and studied her face. She cried even harder now. He barked orders to his soldiers. Two men nodded and ran out of the jail. Soon they returned with an old stretcher. They loaded the woman onto it as she writhed in pain. After more urgent commands, they rushed her through the door of the jail.

The general didn't follow. Instead, he made numerous phone calls. He shouted and paced. After a string of unsuccessful calls, he threw his cell to the ground and raged at the one remaining guard left there. Tom heard the Spanish word for doctor, and from the general's urgent tone, he sensed they needed to rustle one up pretty quick to help the woman.

The general continued to yell at the guard, who cowered near Tom's cell.

"What are you looking at, Frye?" the general said. "This is not a show." He banged on the bars of the cell with his rifle and Tom flinched. The general paced back and forth.

"I'm sorry. Is that your daughter? The pregnant girl."

The general whirled back around to face Tom. "You fool. She is one of my women. And she needs a doctor. Now."

"Oh. Right. Of course."

"I don't have time to deal with you now." The general turned and walked toward the door.

"Wait," Tom called out. "What about a nurse?"

The general stopped walking. He glared at Tom. "What?"

"A nurse. What if you had a nurse helping your ah... girlfriend?"

"Stop your foolishness, man. I need a doctor. Plus, there are no nurses here anyway."

"But there is one." Tom pointed across the room to Mina's cell. "Right there."

CHAPTER 25

The general ran to Mina. "You. Woman. Is this true? You are a nurse?"

She glared at the general before answering, "What if I am? Why should I help your little friend?"

"Mina," Tom said. "Be reasonable. I mean, didn't you take the Hippocratic Oath or something? As a nurse, aren't you morally obligated to help people?"

"Doctors take the Hippocratic Oath, you idiot. I took the Nightingale Pledge, named after Florence Nightingale, the founder of modern nursing."

"Yeah, okay. Same difference, right? Didn't you have to swear to help people?"

The general unlocked Mina's cell and dragged her out. "You! You will help."

Mina crossed her arms. "On two conditions."

"You will not make demands. I am in charge. Not you."

Mina barked back at the general, "Nevertheless, I have two demands."

"What? What are these demands?"

"First, I want decent food if I'm being held prisoner. Nothing with insects in it. And second, I want some of my favorite candy, Swedish Fish."

"Swedish Fish? What is that? Like from the ocean?"

"No, no, no. It's candy. My favorite food in the world, and I haven't had any for almost a week. The cravings are terrible."

Puzzled, the general looked to Tom for clarification. "You understand this fish she speaks of?"

Tom nodded. "Yes. It's a red candy—chewy and shaped like a fish. Kinda like a gumdrop. Very popular. They're delicious." *Oh, man. I could go for some of those myself.* The mere thought of the chewy, delicious candy made him drool.

The general puzzled over the odd requests. After a brief consultation with his cell phone, he nodded. "All right. I will try to find these fish for you."

Hmm, probably looking to see if he can find Swedish Fish on the black market.

Mina chided, "Very well. Oh, and one more thing." She pointed over to Tom. "I want him to assist."

"Me? I'm no doctor. I faint at the sight of blood."

"Weren't you there when your children were born?"

"Yeah, but..."

Looking angry the general unlocked Tom's cell, too. "You, Frye. You will help. Nothing must happen to my Lupe. Or our baby. *Vamos*, we go now to Lupe."

***

They hustled to the other side of the camp until they arrived at one of the nicer looking buildings on the compound. Tom surmised this might be where the upper echelon of the general's henchmen lived. Four generators hummed, pumping electricity into the building. An ample garden stood a few yards away, and Tom noticed a couple of chickens running in the yard.

The building appeared to be divided into four separate apartments. They traversed down a long hallway and entered the last apartment on the left. Once inside the spacious dwelling, they found Lupe laying on a small bed in a back bedroom. Several women tended her, and one sponged her face and neck with water from an old basin. The women clucked like hens when the general entered with Tom and Mina. Tom recognized at least one of them as someone who had served him meals in the jail. *I guess they're surprised to see us out.*

Lupe groaned and the general patted her hand. "You help my Lupe," the general said to his prisoners. "What do we do now?"

Mina scanned the room and addressed the general. "Do you have running water here?"

"Yes."

"Good. Do any of these women speak English?"

"Not so good."

"You'll have to stay, then. To translate," Mina said. "I'll need to give her instructions, and it won't do any good if she can't understand me."

The general frowned but nodded. "Yes. I have calls to make. I'll be back as soon as possible."

"You're not going anywhere before I get what I need," Mina barked. She pointed to the group of women who hovered in the room. "Tell them I need boiling water, clean towels, soap, ice chips for Lupe and scissors."

Tom watched Mina taking charge of the situation with fascination. *She's in the zone, man. Look at her bossing these people around. Everyone has a task. Even the general.*

After translating, the worker bees scurried to produce the goods. Then the general left the makeshift maternity ward, closing the door behind him.

"Thank God, they have electricity and running water," Tom said, looking up at the ceiling fan turning above them. "Otherwise, this room would be an oven."

"Indeed. That horrible general better be making calls to get me my Swedish Fish. That's the only reason I'm doing this. But I'll need to wash my hands before I do anything with her. God knows nothing is sterile here."

Tom raised an eyebrow. "Yeah, right. What do you want me to do?"

"Nothing right now," Mina said.

She left the room and went into the bathroom next door. Tom heard the water running and fantasized about using the restroom himself. *Running water. Flush toilet.*

When she came back, the other women followed her in, bringing the supplies she had demanded. Mina addressed Tom, "I need to determine how far along she is." She looked Lupe in the eye and spoke as she lifted the sheet back. "I'm going to examine you now." Lupe looked terrified as Mina poked and prodded her. She continued to moan, but she cooperated. Apparently, despite the language barrier, she understood Mina wanted to help deliver the baby.

Terrified of seeing anything, Tom turned his back to give Lupe some privacy. "Let me know when you're finished," he said. *I'm feeling queasy already.*

"Don't be ridiculous. You're going to have to assist. I'd say she's seven centimeters dilated," Mina said, pouring some of the hot water into the basin. She washed her hands thoroughly and dried them with a towel.

Lupe suffered another contraction, and Mina barked, "Thomas, go sit near her head until the general gets back. Hold her hand."

Tom noticed a fair amount of blood pooling on the bed, and quickly looked away. He pulled a chair over and sat next to Lupe and took her hand. "Do I need to wash them first?"

"No, you idiot. Hold her hand."

Lupe held onto him like her life depended on it. Tom grimaced. *Okay, this is still better than being in a jail cell. Maybe this will work in our favor.*

"Thomas, show her how to breathe out." Mina scowled when Tom looked confused. "You know, to blow when there are contractions," she explained.

"You mean like that natural childbirth crap?"

"For God's sake, man. Yes."

So, Tom puffed out his cheeks like a blowfish, exaggerating through pantomime how to breathe through a contraction.

Lupe caught on quickly, and Tom breathed through every contraction with her.

This continued for an hour or so, and Tom imagined several bones in his hand had gotten crushed. He feared he might pass out from the heat and the stress. But he fed Lupe ice chips when instructed and helped her through.

Tom and Mina heard a loud ruckus in the hallway, and the general burst into the room carrying several large bags of Swedish Fish, two sandwiches and bottles of water. Tom jumped up to offer his chair. The general tossed a bag of candy to Mina who washed up again, and ripped the bag open to grab a handful. Surprisingly, she passed the bag to the men. Each took some and chewed in silence.

"You found the Swedish Fish, general? How'd you manage that?" Tom asked.

"Never mind. How is Lupe? When will the baby be here?"

Mina washed her hands a third time and looked under the sheet again to measure Lupe's progress. "She's getting close. I think the head should be crowning soon."

"How do you know all this stuff, Mina?" Tom asked.

"How do I know what stuff?"

"About crowning and breathing and dilation. That stuff."

"I'll have you know I was a labor and delivery nurse for twelve years before I married Sam. I've done this thousands of times."

"Well, it looks like our lucky day then, General," Tom said and slapped the man lightly on the back.

"Don't touch me, you fool," the general said, moving closer to Lupe's bed.

Tom opened his mouth to say something, but Lupe let out a blood curdling scream. All three of her visitors jumped in alarm. She pulled on the general's arm, spewing a stream of unrecognizable Spanish.

"She thinks something is wrong." The general's voice rose, trying to talk over Lupe's screams.

Mina tended to her patient again, examining her and looking for signs that she had progressed. She took her pulse. "She needs to push now. I see the baby's head." Mina looked at the general. "You need to tell her that she must push when the next contraction comes. They should come quickly now."

The general leaned close to Lupe and whispered the instructions. She grabbed his hand and nodded, and then screamed again.

"Tell her to push now," Mina yelled.

Lupe pushed and pushed until she was red in the face. Mina encouraged her and they all coached her through the rapid onset of contractions. This continued for long minutes which became two hours, with Lupe screaming and pushing and everyone cheering her on. But she grew weaker with every contraction. She refused the ice chips Tom offered her.

"Thomas, I need you to scrub in. I may need your help."

"Me? What do you mean?"

"Go wash your hands with warm water. Be thorough. I need you to assist."

"But why?"

"The head is sliding in and out," Mina said. "I think the cord is wrapped around the baby's neck."

CHAPTER 26

Tom ran to the bathroom and washed his hands, scrubbing thoroughly up beyond his elbows. *All those television doctors scrub in for at least five minutes, right? How long does it take to kill these germs? Maybe the soap has already been contaminated with Salvadoran germs. My immune system will recognize them as foreign, and I'll catch some freakish disease.*

He wondered if he should give it one more round with the soap and water, when Mina's loud voice trumpeted down the hall.

"Thomas. Now."

"Coming." Tom wiped his hands on the questionable hand towel. He cringed but returned to help.

Lupe moaned, but appeared to have lost the strength to push. The general positioned himself beside her head and held her hand. Mina kept the area as clean as possible, tossing aside soiled towels and blankets onto a heap on the floor. The worker bees picked them up and whisked them out of the room, bringing clean replacements.

"General," Mina said. "Tell her that she must push when the next contraction comes. While she pushes, I have to see if I can feel the cord wrapped around the baby's neck."

The general nodded, whispering instructions to Lupe. Meanwhile, Tom thought he might throw up. *I would so rather be battling sea sickness than doing this.*

"Thomas," Mina said. "Look alive. I need you to be down here, too. It may take both of us to do this. You will have to catch the baby while I remove the cord. Got it?"

"I'm afraid I'll faint."

"Nonsense! You cannot faint. I forbid it. I need you to help me deliver this baby. Now pull yourself together. Act like a man. And for the time being, you work on the breathing with Lupe."

Terrified of opening his mouth and spewing vomit all over the patient, Tom nodded and tried to remain calm. He focused on Lupe, encouraging her to breathe through the contractions.

Lupe moaned as another contraction enveloped her in pain. Mina continued to coach her, and the general translated, telling her to push long and hard.

"Thomas, get down here. I'm going to insert my hand to see what I can feel. Before I do, I want you to look at the baby's head. Do you see it?"

Tom bent down and peered under the sheet at the tiny, dark head, trying to exit its mother. "Okay, I see it." He tried not to focus on the vast amount of blood and the smell emanating from the bed.

Lupe yelled what sounded like Spanish curse words as Mina poked and probed. The general and Tom each took a side and pinned Lupe's arms so she wouldn't struggle. But she didn't have much fight left. With each push, she grew weaker and less capable of sustaining the energy to push the baby out.

"I've got my fingers on the cord. It's wrapped at least twice around the baby's neck. I won't be able to get it off until the head is fully out. Tell her what's happening, general."

The general spoke softly to Lupe, but her eyes, red and glazed, lacked comprehension. "I don't think she understands."

"You need to make her understand," Mina said. "Her baby's life, and her life, depend on it. Tell her she must push, or her baby will die."

***

Tom lost track of time. With every contraction, he readied himself to assist in the birth, but the baby didn't come. He realized the gravity of the situation. *I'm gonna do whatever Mina tells me. To help Lupe. And to save the baby.* But there was so much blood.

"The baby is in distress," Mina said. "She's got to push harder than she ever has."

Now the general's pleas to Lupe sounded more like a command. Despite the language barrier, everyone got the message. They cheered her on and rallied her to push.

When Lupe's next contraction came, Lupe absorbed the energy of her caregivers and pushed with all her might.

"Thomas, quick. Be ready to grab the baby. The head is out."

"Aaaah!" Lupe screamed.

After the head emerged, Mina held on with one hand as her other hand guided the shoulders. With the shoulders out, she instructed Tom while she wrestled to free the baby's neck from the Nuchal cord.

"Thomas, the cord is in a locked pattern—like a knot around the baby's neck. Quickly, general! Bring me the scissors."

Tom held the baby as Mina tugged at the cord making a quick snip.

"Give me the baby." Mina laid the newborn on Lupe's chest and quickly loosened the cord, freeing the baby. She picked up the baby again, giving it a quick slap, urging it to breathe.

"What is it? Boy or girl?" the general asked.

But Mina ignored him, focusing instead on the task at hand. She used her index finger to clear out the baby's mouth and nose and tried again. She put her head to the tiny baby's nose and mouth and listened. She patted the baby's back again. Without a response, Mina put the baby on a small, flat bedside table and blew two gentle puffs of air into its lungs. She listened, then repeated the gesture. One last time, she patted the baby's back firmly and at last a cry rang out in the room.

"Oh, thank God," Mina said.

Tom found himself close to tears. The general sighed and hugged Lupe. Mina cleaned the baby and put her on Lupe's chest.

"Congratulations," Mina said. "It's a girl."

CHAPTER 27

Mina and Tom tended to Lupe while the general held his daughter. Tom had forgotten the grisly details of childbirth after his two girls were born. The smell of blood permeated the room, and with so many people in the small space, it made Tom queasy. But Tom still allowed Mina to boss him around. He had to hand it to her. She knew her stuff.

After the afterbirth delivered and Mina cleaned Lupe up, the ladies came back to tidy the room with fresh linens. The vast differences in housing conditions baffled Tom. The prisoners and most of the workers lived a peasant lifestyle, yet the general's little love nest appeared to have all the creature comforts. *For a prison camp, they sure have a lot of clean sheets and towels.* He shuddered thinking about the filthy cot he'd lain on the past several days. It made his skin crawl. But at least they'd stayed alive.

Although the general looked smitten with his baby, he grew bored quickly and barked orders to one of the women to take his daughter. "I must get back to work. And you two... I still need to deal with you."

Tom's stomach flip-flopped. The general had acted like a regular father during the birthing ordeal. Now they circled back to square one.

Mina wiped her forehead with the back of her palm, decorating it with a fresh swipe of red. Tom noticed Mina's face splattered with blood. Lupe's blood was all over her clothing; Tom's too.

Mina spoke first. "Lupe needs medical attention, General. She's lost a great deal of blood. And the baby should be examined by a physician immediately."

The general studied Mina and Tom before he answered. Then he looked at Lupe and the baby. The woman had passed out, dead tired. The baby slept too, no doubt exhausted from the ordeal. "They look fine to me."

"Are you a doctor?" Mina barked, back to her feisty self. "After all we did to save them both, you can't take the chance. There could be complications. Lupe had a difficult delivery. And the baby must be examined right away. Can you get them to a hospital?"

The general looked at Tom. "Can I trust her? Is she telling the truth?"

"Yes," Tom agreed, nodding his head. "They need to see a doctor."

"This is my first child," the general said.

Then it clicked in Tom's head. The general didn't know what to do.

"The women in our camp, they use the midwife from the closest village. If there are problems, well..." The general's voice trailed off.

"You let them die?" Mina asked. "You animal."

"It is God's decision who lives and dies, not mine," the general said.

"General, you never had a reason to think about this before. But now..." Tom said.

The general scowled and pointed his finger at Mina. "You, woman. You have made things difficult. I had planned to make contact with your husband yesterday." He waved his hands in the air, gesturing to Lupe and his baby. "Before all this happened."

"I saved her life. Both of their lives, but they need a doctor. She is hemorrhaging. Don't be a fool."

The general leaned in toward Mina and raised his hand. He stopped short of hitting her and paced the floor instead. The shouting woke Lupe, who gasped and struggled to sit up, reaching for her baby. The baby started to cry adding tension to an already stressful situation.

"The baby needs to nurse," Mina said. She put the baby in Lupe's arms and instructed her with body language.

"I will send someone to find a doctor," the general said. "Then I will deal with the two of you. Come now. Back to your cells."

Both Tom and Mina looked dejected. "Can we clean up first?" Tom said, looking down at his hands and fingernails, caked with blood.

The general sniffed, annoyed with the request. "Make it quick." He opened the door and yelled for the guards.

They each had a chance to wash their face and hands under the watch of guards. Then they were ushered back to their concrete prison cells.

***

Prospects looked grim, back in jail and locked in their individual cells. Devastated, Tom called across to Mina. "What are we going to do now? I thought maybe he'd let us go."

"He'll kill us. I'm sure of it," Mina said.

"Not necessarily. If he gets through to the ship... if they get ahold of Sam and Vicky, we still have a chance."

"We're doomed," Mina said. "That man has no conscience. He's a ruthless killer."

"Yes. But he's never been a father before."

"What difference will that make?" Mina lay on her cot. "I'm exhausted. I need to rest."

Tom thought he heard her crying. *God, I never thought I'd see Mina so vulnerable. This could be it. The end of the road for both of us.* He closed his eyes tight and knelt on the dirt floor, praying the same simple mantra—*Please, Lord. Save us.*

CHAPTER 28

The rustling of Mina's bag of Swedish Fish woke Tom. *I guess I dozed off.* He had a crick in his neck and his legs prickled with needles and pins. *How long have I been asleep? Too bad that psycho general stole my watch.* Standing proved more difficult than he imagined, but once the circulation returned to his legs, he pushed himself off the floor. *I hope this is the last time I fall asleep kneeling on a dirt floor.*

Mina stopped eating her candy and walked to the door of her cell. "How on earth could you fall asleep like that? Your snoring woke me."

"Yeah well, your noisy candy bag woke me, so I guess we're even. Any idea what time it is?"

"They haven't brought our evening ration of gruel yet, so I'm guessing it's not too late."

"At least you have your Swedish Fish. I'm surprised he let you bring them back with you."

"I put them down my pants," Mina said.

"Well, that's a visual I won't soon forget."

"Indeed. You pervert."

"You could share them with me. I did help deliver the baby."

"A monkey could've done what you did."

"Hey now..." *Again, with the monkey jokes.*

Mina chomped and rumpled the bag, now making as much noise as she could. Tom paced in his cell, trying to ignore his growling stomach. Bone tired, he envied Mina her candy.

Instead he focused on where he imagined the cruise ship would be. From what he remembered of the ship's itinerary this should be the last day at sea. Tomorrow the Oceanos would dock in the port of San Diego, California. *Boy, I'd give anything to be back in the states again.*

Tom fantasized that Vicky and Dr. Stab were in negotiations with the United States Embassy, or the Merchant Marines or the Coast Guard. *Had this disaster developed into an international news event? Wouldn't that be something?* Most of all he wondered if anyone was searching for them. *They must be looking. Jesus H. Christ. What a mess.* He kept walking the cell, determined to fight the anxiety.

A short time later, two women arrived with their evening meal. On tonight's menu was a portion of meat, some beans and a piece of crusty bread. The bread, a new addition to their usual meals, tasted delicious. *Good. Carbohydrates for energy. Thank God.* Tom chewed slowly, savoring every bite. *This prison food has improved. No doubt about it. Score one for Mina and her demands.*

The women waited for Tom and Mina to finish their meal, and then collected the dirty dishes. "I demand to see the general," Mina said to the woman who took her plate.

"General. He busy. He no here."

"What do you mean, he's not here?"

"He go to find doctor for Lupe and baby."

Tom and Mina exchanged a look from across the small jail. *How interesting. They seem to speak and understand English when it suits them.* Tom decided to put in his two cents worth. "When he gets back, could you ask him to come talk to us?"

The women nodded their heads and scurried outside. After the door closed behind them, Tom called out to Mina, "Hey, that's good, right? He listened to you. He's looking for a doctor."

"I suppose so. Let's hope he finds one soon. Before it's too late for Lupe."

"And for us."

Within moments, the general burst through the door with two guards. The guards unlocked the cells and dragged them out.

"You will come with me now. I brought a doctor from the port. He is examining Lupe and our daughter now. He wishes to speak with you both."

"The port? You mean Acajutla?" Tom tried to hide the excitement in his voice.

"Yes. Why?"

"Uh, no reason. I figured that would take a long time to get there and back, that's all." *We must be closer to the port than I thought.*

Once outside, Tom's eyes took a moment to adjust to the twilight. Soon the pitch-black night would envelop the camp. As they walked past the latrine, the guards paused to see if they needed to use it.

"Could we use the bathroom in the apartment?" Mina said. "Please?"

The guards looked to the general for confirmation. He nodded and started walking again. *Damn, woman. You've got balls.*

They arrived at the apartment building. "Hurry up. No more wasting time," the general said. "I will use the toilet first. Then you two."

The general took his time, making the two prisoners wait. Finally, he came out and Mina scurried in before Tom had the chance. When she'd finished, the general grabbed Mina by the elbow and pulled her into Lupe's room. "You. Woman. Come with me. Frye, make it quick. I need to talk to the doctor."

Tom used the facilities and ran the water, preparing to wash up. Something shiny glinted under the hand towel on the edge of the sink. Tentatively he lifted the towel, wondering if the general had left a knife or other weapon behind. But no. There it was. His stolen watch! Possibly the last gift from his precious wife. Carefully he dried it with the towel and put it in his pocket. *Oh, is this a good idea?* Christ. If the general caught him with it, he'd be punished. God knows how. But dammit, it was his watch. He made up his mind to take the risk. Quickly he finished cleaning up and left the bathroom. Tom knocked tentatively and entered Lupe's room just as the doctor was wrapping up his examination. The doctor looked young. He pulled off his latex gloves in a quick fluid motion.

"General, considering what Lupe and the baby have suffered, they are stable. But I recommend taking them to the hospital in Acajutla immediately. Lupe may need a transfusion, and your daughter..." The doctor paused, reflecting. "I cannot be sure the child is healthy. Given the circumstances. She should be examined more thoroughly."

"That is out of the question," the general said.

"They could die."

Silence hung in the air. Tom held his breath, wondering what would happen next. *How can we convince him? If Lupe or the baby dies, the general will kill us for sure.*

"We delivered the baby, doctor." Tom pointed to Mina and himself. "Well, Mina did most of it. I assisted."

"Ah, the general owes you a debt of gratitude then, my friends," the doctor said with a sad smile. "They both would have died if you had not helped." He walked to Lupe's bedside and took her wrist to check her pulse. "Lupe told me what happened. That the cord was wrapped around her daughter's neck. How you saved them both."

Mina waved her hand in front of her face. "As a nurse, I'm obligated to help. I did what I could." She looked at Tom. "I didn't do it alone. Tom helped."

"Nevertheless, you are both to be commended." The doctor turned to face the general, who stood scowling in a far corner of the room. "General, I agreed to come here. To tend to your woman, your child. But I beg you sir, take them to the hospital."

The general stormed out of the room, slamming the door behind him. Lupe, Tom, Mina and the doctor looked at one another, unsure of what would happen next.

"My friends," the doctor said. "I'm not sure what circumstances have brought you here. In this horrible place. To help with the baby's delivery." No one spoke, so the doctor continued. "Are you here against your will?"

"Kidnapped from the market at Acajutla," Tom confirmed. "Held for ransom. But as far as we know, the general hasn't contacted our families. Not yet, anyway."

A bitter laugh erupted from Mina. "Not yet. Not ever. He's going to kill us."

"Don't say that, Mina."

"Tell me, Doctor," Mina said. "Did they bring you here against *your* will?"

The doctor shook his head. "No. I agreed to come."

Tom and Mina looked puzzled. "Really?" Tom asked.

Nodding his head, the doctor looked down at his shoes. "I have ties. To this organization, MS 13. I am ashamed to admit it, but my brother is involved in the gang. I keep in contact with him. Although I do not support his ideals."

The doctor explained that the group had sprung from one of the street gangs formed in the 1980s in the United States by children of Salvadoran immigrants who'd fled their homeland during the civil war. In the early 2000s, they spread to Central America and formed out of a corrupt government and utilized former military and integrated police to assist them. Their specialties were kidnapping, human trafficking, extortion and drug smuggling.

"You see, this Northern Triangle—Honduras, Nicaragua, and Guatemala—they use the port of Acajutla to smuggle arms and drugs, because of El Salvador's short coastline. It makes it far too easy. Mainly these are run through two transport networks, the Perrones and Texis Cartels. And the government is so corrupt. The prisons are run by the gangs. Violence and justice are synonymous in Central America."

"So, your brother is part of this?" Tom said.

"Yes. He is one of the general's top lieutenants. We have agreed to disagree about justice. Our father fought on the right side of the civil war. He died in a prison camp, very much like this place. My brother and I were babies when that happened. I chose to study hard, to become a doctor. Help people. But my brother sought revenge."

"My God," Tom said. "What a story."

The doctor's cell phone buzzed in his pocket. "Excuse me, please." The doctor walked to the other side of the room, speaking quietly into his phone. After a few moments, he returned, placing his cell phone on the windowsill. He smiled and pulled up a chair next to Lupe's bed and removed his laptop from his duffle bag on the floor near Lupe's bed. "I need to make a few notes."

"Notes?" Tom asked.

The doctor nodded. "I'm hopeful the general will come to his senses. I want to document the details of the birth, and the treatment administered to Lupe in your care. Then, if... No, when she gets to the hospital, I will have all the information to give to the medical team."

Tired of sitting in the uncomfortable wooden chairs Tom and Mina had been parked in for hours, he walked to the window, yanking up the noisy blinds. No one appeared to pay any attention. *Okay, Tom-O. It's now or never.* He stood at the window looking out at the black sky. Except for the doctor's typing, everything remained quiet. *Do it. Go ahead. You have nothing to lose.* His heart pounded.

Then, without warning, Mina sprang from her seat. "Aha! Yes," she said. She hurried to the dresser beside Lupe's bed. "Now I remember." She pulled two bags of candy from the dresser drawers. "I remember seeing the general put the rest of my Swedish Fish in here. She stuffed one of the bags in her trousers and the other down the back of her shirt.

Tom threw her a disgusted look, and the doctor raised an eyebrow in surprise.

"Ignore her," Tom said. "She's obsessed with the Swedish Fish candy. Her reward for delivering the baby."

Mina ripped open one of the bags and stuffed a couple of fish into her mouth, talking with her mouth full. "I worked hard for these. Leave me alone." She settled into a corner of the room and sat on the floor.

"Doctor, do you think we'll get out of here? Alive?" Tom asked.

"I don't know. I'm not sure anyone in this room will get out alive." The doctor pointed to Lupe who cradled her baby and dozed. "But I think time is running out." He resumed his work, clicking away on his keyboard.

"Umm, doctor. Is it all right if I use the restroom?" Tom asked.

"You don't have to ask *me* for permission."

"Excuse me," Tom said walking toward the door. "I'll be right back."

The doctor nodded, continuing to type his patient notes while Mina scarfed down Swedish Fish.

Tom walked past the guards to the bathroom, then locked the door behind him and pulled the doctor's cell phone out of his pocket. He took a deep breath, praying for a signal, then punched in Vicky's number for a text message.

Vicky, it's me. I had the chance to steal this phone for a minute. We're ok. Still in El Salvador, kidnapped somewhere outside Acajutla. Call the police! I love you and the girls. XO Tom.

He hit send and then wondered how to call the police. Was 911 used internationally? *Shit! Think, Tom.* He seemed to remember JJ rattling off the instructions to call for help in Central America. *What did he say? Oh, wait. I know now. It's 112. I remember thinking, oh, okay. I can remember that. Like one plus one is two.*

Holding his breath, he dialed 112 and waited. Sure enough, after a couple of rings, a man's voice answered in Spanish. Tom struggled. He didn't know any Spanish. After a few seconds, he caved and resorted to English. "Hello! Help me! Help! I've been kidnapped by someone called the general outside Acajutla!"

CHAPTER 29

The doctor examined Lupe again while Mina and Tom looked on. "She's lost so much blood. I'm certain now she needs a transfusion." He whispered to her and she grabbed his wrist. They spoke briefly, but neither Tom nor Mina understood what they said.

Lupe sat up abruptly. "*Clerigo. Clerigo.*"

"What is she saying?" Tom asked.

"She is asking for a priest," the doctor replied.

"Jesus, Mary and Joseph."

"Yes. They would be helpful also," the doctor said with a sad smile. "She is asking for last rights. And for the baby to be baptized. She thinks she is going to die."

"Well, where are we going to find a priest?" Mina sounded annoyed.

"It's not too likely, I guess," Tom agreed.

"Don't be so sure, my friends," the doctor said. "Priests are on the payroll, too."

"That's disgusting," Tom said.

"Yes. But that is the way of our world, friend," the doctor said. "Tell me, please. What are your names?"

"I'm Tom Frye. And this is Mina Stab."

"Stab? Like with a sword?"

Tom chuckled. "Yes. Exactly like that."

"Honestly," Mina said. "I don't find anything about this conversation amusing."

"Lupe asked me when I first arrived if I knew your names. Now I can tell her. I am Pablo." The doctor leaned closed to Lupe and pointed to Tom and Mina. "*Señor Tomas y señora Mina.*"

Lupe looked over and smiled. She stretched out her hand to Mina with her free arm. In her other arm, she held her daughter fast.

Mina left the candy behind and sat on the edge of Lupe's bed. Lupe took Mina's hand in hers and kissed it. Tom felt tears springing to his eyes and a lump rising in his throat.

"Now, now. You're going to be fine," Mina whispered to Lupe. "Doctor, tell her."

The doctor spoke in low tones to Lupe who shook her head. "*Clerigo.*"

"I will go look for the general," the doctor said. "We must do something, or she will die."

Long minutes ticked by as they waited for someone to return. Tom looked out the window at the dark night sky. In the distance, he spotted some campfires, but the compound had grown quiet and eerie. Then, in the distance he heard the loud, thumping beat of a helicopter. *Maybe we're going to be rescued.*

"Mina," he whispered. "Do you hear that? It sounds like a helicopter."

She jumped from her seat on the floor and ran to the window. "You're right. But I can't see it."

"Do you think it's here for us?" Tom asked.

"I wouldn't get my hopes up if I were you."

"Well, it sounds like it's getting close."

Lupe moaned. *She must hear the helicopter, too.* The baby stirred in Lupe's arms, but remained quiet. *That worries me more than anything. That baby hardly cries.* Then they saw the lights from the chopper as it flew over the building. Tom grabbed onto Mina's arm and squeezed it. "Look."

"Get your hands off me, you savage," Mina said.

"For God's sake. The helicopter landed. It's gotta be here for us."

"*Hmm.*" Mina took another large handful of Swedish Fish. "I'll believe it when we're in the sky."

A short time later, the general, the doctor and another man burst through the door. The general hustled to Lupe's bedside and waved over the doctor and the other man. As they got closer, Tom saw the clerical collar. A priest. *Holy shit.*

The priest removed a small leather satchel from his bag and extracted his tools. He produced a miniature bottle of holy water, a jar of sacramental oil and a box of eucharist wafers.

The priest, the general and Lupe talked amongst themselves. Then the priest pointed to Tom and Mina and spoke to them in English. "You two. You will stand in as witnesses. Since there are no godparents."

"But I'm not even Catholic," Tom said. "Isn't that against the law, or something?"

"This is an emergency. Are you both baptized Christians?"

Tom and Mina nodded.

"Then you will have to do. *Señora*, you will hold the child." He handed the baby to Mina. Tom stood next to her.

The priest conducted the brief baptism ceremony. He spoke in Spanish, so Tom and Mina didn't comprehend much beyond the basics. The priest poured water over the baby's head and announced her name.

"Thomasina Mina," the priest declared and then instructed Mina to hand the child to Lupe. Stunned, Mina narrowly escaped dropping the child.

"Excuse me. What did you say?" Tom asked.

The priest ignored Tom's question and transitioned to the next sacrament, the anointing of the sick. He focused his attention on Lupe and the tiny baby in her arms.

"Did he say, 'Thomasina Mina'?"

Since no one else spoke, the doctor answered, "Yes. Lupe wanted to name the baby after you both. You brought her into the world."

Stunned, Tom let the news sink in before speaking again. "And the general... he's okay with this?"

The doctor frowned. "Ah, no. But it is the child's mother's wish. He can argue the point later. When Lupe and the baby have recovered."

"Well, I for one am offended," Mina said. "I did all the hard work. My name should be first."

"For God's sake, Mina. It doesn't matter," Tom said.

"Well, it does to me." Mina stormed off and returned to her corner with the Swedish Fish.

"Doctor, do you think the general is willing to take Lupe and the baby to the hospital? I mean, he helicoptered in a priest. Why won't he get them emergency medical care?"

"I'm still trying to persuade him. He is a stubborn man. Perhaps Father will convince him."

After the priest had performed the anointing, he and the general left the room. On his way out, the general invited the doctor to join them. A short time later, two women came into the room. One tended to Lupe and the baby, while the other packed a suitcase with some clothes and baby supplies.

"Mina, look! I think they're packing Lupe's things. They must be planning to take her to the hospital."

"You might be right, Thomas." Mina hid the candy bag in her pants again and stood. She gestured to the women. "Looks like they're in a hurry."

A few moments later, two paramedics entered the room with a stretcher. The doctor and the general looked on, conversing amongst themselves as the paramedics moved Lupe to the stretcher. Then they moved the baby to an infant carrier, which the general grabbed.

"You're taking them to the hospital? Good," Tom said.

As he held his daughter's carrier, the general stared at Tom and Mina. Outside, they still heard the night air humming with the buzz from the chopper blades. Rushing past them, paramedics whisked Lupe out of the bedroom.

The general walked to the doorway but stopped and turned around to look at his prisoners. "This has not turned out the way I planned." Then he barked orders to two guards stationed by the door. "Take them." He walked away without looking back again.

CHAPTER 30

The guards marched Tom and Mina out of the prison barracks and forced them into an old army jeep at gunpoint. One of them kept his gun cocked and aimed at their heads, while the other blindfolded them. After forcing them to stay seated in the back, the jeep took off into the pitch-black night, bouncing along the bumpy back roads. Tom swore he heard his own heart pounding, knowing with every jolt of the jeep, the unsecured gun could fire.

No one uttered a word. Mina reached out and grabbed his hand, squeezing it tight, and Tom squeezed back. *This could be it. The end of the road. How crazy to think I could be facing death with Mina, of all people. Someone I once despised. Yet here we are together. God help us.*

Blindfolded, Tom had no sense of direction. He tried to listen carefully for any sounds that might give him a clue to his surroundings, but the grinding gears of the jeep made it impossible to hear anything. They bounced along the rough roads, plowing through potholes and ditches. He and Mina thrashed in the back seat. Tom lost all track of time, not knowing how long or far they'd traveled. But the temperature in the open-air vehicle changed. A cool breeze blew through his hair. He sniffed and the air smelled different.

The sea. It smells like the ocean. Are we getting closer to the water? God, maybe they're going to drown us. I want to scream, dammit, but I can't. I've got to keep silent. Tom clutched Mina's hand tighter and prayed silently for help.

Overcome with panic, and vulnerable, he struggled to keep his composure. *If I'm going to die, I'm not going to die like a coward.*

The jeep screeched to a halt, and the soldiers climbed out and opened the back doors. Yanking Tom and Mina from the backseat they ordered them to start walking. Still blindfolded, the prisoners stumbled along while the guards prodded them with the ends of their rifles. Tom stretched out his hands in front of him, grasping at nothing in the night, shuffling in tiny steps. When they both fell, tripping over one another, the guards laughed and offered no help to stand.

After walking a hundred yards or so, the guards ordered them to stop and knocked them down onto the damp grass. Tom's knees and elbows throbbed from the many falls he'd had along the way. At least this was a soft landing. *God, this must be the end of the road for me. They're going to shoot us. And throw our bodies into the ocean. I'll never see Vicky or the girls again.* He choked back tears, determined to stay brave. Mina sobbed openly. *She knows, too. We're dead.*

The guards removed the blindfolds, then stood over their prisoners. They smirked and chuckled. "Okay, *gringos.* Listen up," the driver said. "This is where we leave you."

"Leave us? What do you mean?" Tom asked.

"Where are we? We're in the middle of nowhere," Mina said.

"No *señora*, you are not," the second guard said. "You are close to the port."

"The port? Acajutla?" Tom asked.

"*Si*, you can walk from here. But you must wait until you hear the signal from us."

The guards both laughed. "Move before you hear the signal, and we will shoot you," the driver said.

"You mean you're setting us free?" Mina gasped.

"That is what the general commands. By delivering Lupe's baby, you have earned your freedom."

"Also, the woman is a pain in the ass," the second guard said. They both chuckled.

"Honestly, I've never—" Mina said.

Tom cut her off. "So, we're free?"

"Yes. When you hear the signal, you can go."

"Signal? What signal? And how will we know which way to go?" Mina asked.

"*Adios.*" The guards gave a mocking salute and walked away. The driver shouted back to them, "Follow the road, *señora*. You will get there."

Within a few minutes, they heard the jeep start up and the sound of one solitary gunshot.

"I guess that's our signal," Tom said. "Let's start walking." He offered Mina a hand to help her stand.

"You'd think they could've dropped us off closer than this," Mina complained. "This whole ordeal has been atrocious."

"But Mina, we're free! They've let us go. The port can't be too far."

Tom's mind whirred thinking back to his frantic phone call to the authorities from the doctor's phone, and the text he sent to his wife. *Maybe the message got through to Vicky after all. And what if the authorities managed to track down the general? Maybe—if they could hone in on the phone's GPS...*

"Well, it's about time they let us go. Big help you were."

"Hey, now. It's your fault we got into this mess. You're the one who stole my idol."

"I beg your pardon. If you'd have handed it over, and been chivalrous, we would not be in this predicament."

Tom started to get annoyed but tried to suppress it. "Let's get moving. It'll take us longer in the dark. I'm not sure what time it is, but I'd guess it's a couple of hours until daybreak."

They moved along the dark road cautiously. Whenever they heard a loud noise, they both startled and moved toward each other. Terrified, Mina opted to cling onto Tom's sleeve.

"I have night blindness, Thomas. You have to guide me."

"I'm not your seeing eye dog, Mina. Keep up."

Tom still couldn't believe the odds of him and Mina being marooned on a small island together. *We've been kidnapped, missed our ship, held hostage, imprisoned, interrogated and beaten. On top of all that, we delivered a baby, saved the lives of both mother and child, and had a baby named after us. Then, gagged, blindfolded and dropped in the outskirts of a jungle in the middle of the night and left to hobble into a port known to harbor drug lords, kidnappers and corrupt police. You can't make this shit up.*

As they journeyed on, night sounds from the jungle surrounded them. Mysterious animal noises erupted from the trees and bushes, and insects swirled all around.

Mina batted at the mosquitos and complained non-stop. "My feet hurt, Thomas. I need to stop and rest." As if on cue, a loud growl rumbled in the scruffy vegetation growing along the road.

"We keep moving. Did you hear that roar? I prefer not to be that creature's dinner. Come on." Tom pulled her along, determined to make it to the seaport. "We've got to be getting close. Can't you smell the ocean?"

"The only thing I can smell is you and your dirty clothes. And you stink."

"Right back at you, sister. I'd give anything to see your face when you look in the mirror for the first time."

"I'll still look better than you. Even at my worst."

Tom ignored the dig and pulled her along. He entertained the idea of stopping to rest, but where? *Must be safer to keep moving, right? But I'm so tired. I don't think I can walk much further. And I'm dying of thirst.*

When he thought they couldn't go another step, he noticed the sky starting to brighten with the early signs of daylight. Low on the horizon, he saw the promise of the sunrise.

"Mina, the sun is coming up. Look." He pointed to the sky. "Keep going. We've gotta be getting close."

With the daylight, he saw tiny houses speckled in the distance. They'd found the outskirts of town. Right by the craft market where this nightmare started. He recognized this. Yes. They had to be close. Tom dragged Mina, forcing her to keep pace.

It looked like they had made it back to civilization. More houses popped up on regular city streets. Then they spotted a small bodega situated on the corner of an alley.

"Mina, there's a grocery store. But I guess it's too early for anything to be open."

"Maybe we should sit there and wait," Mina said.

In the daytime, Tom saw how bedraggled they looked. *God, we might scare somebody. It's crazy.* The thought made him smile.

"But wait, Thomas. Look, over there. It's a woman. She's wearing scrubs."

They watched a petite woman exit from a side door of the building. Dressed as a nurse, she looked as though she might be headed to work.

"Hey! Hey!" Tom screamed. He and Mina rushed down the tiny side street to catch up with the woman. *God, I wish I could remember the Spanish word for help.*

She stopped and stared, looking puzzled. "*Hola?*"

"Are you a nurse?" Mina asked. "Do you speak English?"

"Yes, and yes," the nurse said. "Do you need help?"

"Do we ever," Tom said.

"Oh, yes. Please help us," Mina said. She collapsed in front of the bodega's front steps.

CHAPTER 31

The nurse, whose family owned the little store where Mina collapsed, called for an ambulance. Mina slowly regained consciousness. The woman brought them both huge glasses of water, which they guzzled. Filthy and covered in insect bites, Tom and Mina waited on the steps for the ambulance and authorities to arrive. While they waited, Tom explained the kidnapping and the bizarre events leading to their subsequent release. As soon as he'd told their story, his hands began to shake.

"How do we know these are the real police that you called?" Tom asked. "I mean, that's how we got into this mess in the first place."

The nurse comforted Tom, patting his hand and looking into his eyes. "I understand you are afraid. But not all police here are corrupt. At the hospital, we know who can be trusted."

When the ambulance and police arrived, the nurse rode with them to the hospital. "Who can I call for you, Mr. Frye? Your wife? It might be a while until you get the chance to contact her."

"Yes, please." Tom rattled off the number for Vicky's cell. *God, I hope she got the text I sent from the doctor's phone so she knows that we're still alive.*

The nurse copied the number and squeezed his hand. "I'll get Mrs. Stab's information as well and contact her husband." She smiled at Tom. "Everything will be all right now. You'll get home to your family." The nurse waved and walked away. "I'll make the calls from the nurse's station. Goodbye."

The emergency room staff treated Tom and Mina and tended to their minor injuries. After the hospital released them, the police, who'd been hanging around, wanted their statements. The authorities escorted them to a conference room in the basement of the hospital where they conducted the interview.

After hearing Tom's and Mina's story, the police confirmed that scams and kidnappings ran rampant in many of the ports where the cruise ships docked. In Acajutla, the general and his associates had notorious reputations. Gangs and drug lords had infiltrated many legitimate businesses—including the police and military.

"They are well known to us, Mr. Frye," the police officer taking Tom's statement said. "The only surprise is that they released you. Alive."

"Yeah, I can't believe it myself. I thought for sure they'd kill us both." Tom ran a hand through his hair. "Honestly, that's what gave me the courage to smuggle the doctor's phone into the bathroom and text my wife."

"Mr. Frye, it was brave of you to do that. It confirmed to us what we had suspected all along. That you and Mrs. Stab were being held by MS 13."

"And you claim that early in the week, the general offered to release you in exchange for Mrs. Stab?"

"Yes. That's correct."

"But you refused? You decided to stay?"

"Yes."

"Can you tell me why?"

"I know Mina Stab. I've known her and her husband, Dr. Sam Stab, for years. I couldn't abandon her. No matter how annoying she can be."

The police officer raised a quizzical eyebrow. "Annoying?"

"It's a long story, officer. We have a history. We go way back."

"Ah. Very well. She was fortunate to have you looking out for her."

"I'm not sure she would agree. But thank you anyway. So, are we almost finished here? I need to get in touch with my family as soon as possible."

"Certainly. But first, let's talk about the general's girlfriend. You believe she and the baby are alive?"

"Yes. At least the last time I saw them. The general whisked them off in a helicopter. With a doctor and a priest."

"Ah, that tells me he took them out of the country. Probably to Panama." The police officer shrugged and leaned closer to Tom, whispering, "Better hospitals."

Tom nodded. "As long as he's not at *this* hospital."

"I can guarantee he is not."

"So, when can I go home? I'm not sure how to go about any of this. I mean, I lost my phone, my wallet, passport. He looked at his wrist and smiled. "Frankly, I can't believe I got my watch back. I thought it was gone for good."

"Leave the details to us, Mr. Frye. After what you've been through, it's the least we can do. We'll get you home. It may take a day or two, but I guarantee it. Your story is international news. You're going to be a celebrity."

"I couldn't care less about being a celebrity. But I'd kill for a shower and some decent food. And to talk to my wife."

"Yes, of course. Let's get you out of here. I believe Mrs. Stab's interview has concluded as well. Let's lock up here and we'll take you to the hotel by the port."

The minute the door opened Tom heard Mina coming down the hall. He and the officer exchanged a curious look.

"What do you mean it'll take a day or two to get us out of this godforsaken country? I demand you telephone the embassy this instant. In fact, I want you to contact the American Embassy and the Swedish Embassy. I'll make this into an international public relations nightmare for this horrible little country."

"Mrs. Stab, we're working as fast as we can," the officer said. "Please. Be patient. Come along now, we'll give you a ride to the hotel."

"Hotel? I want to go home. I demand you take me to the embassy this instant. I'm not spending another unnecessary minute here. Summon a private jet. Immediately."

Tom walked over and tried to intervene. "Mina. Let's get out of this hospital. We can get cleaned up at the hotel. Make some phone calls. I'm sure the embassy has been contacted."

"Indeed. I want to speak with my husband now. Get him on the phone."

"Mina, try to calm down. Come on now."

Mina turned around and began smacking Tom with both fists, beating him on the head and screaming. "You! Thomas. This is all your fault. The whole thing."

"Help! Stop her," Tom yelled.

The police officers each grabbed one of Mina's arms, trying to control her. But she thrashed around like a wild animal.

"Call for backup," the one cop yelled to a paramedic who came around the corner to investigate. "I think we need to sedate her."

CHAPTER 32

Tom stretched out on the hotel bed and closed his eyes. After hearing Vicky's voice on the other end of the phone, he started to believe this nightmare might be over.

The cruise ship, Oceanos, had docked several days before in San Diego, and his family had waited there. They'd refused to travel home without him. In a day, or two at the most, he'd be back in the States and reunited with Vicky and their daughters.

After Mina attacked him, the police escorted Tom and a heavily sedated Mina to the United States Embassy. They secured copies of their passports and got the go ahead to arrange a flight as soon as all the bureaucratic bull had been resolved. But a couple of negotiations promised to speed up the process—the Mayor of Acajutla requested an interview, and then a joint news conference would take place at City Hall in the town square. After that, they'd be flown to San Diego, courtesy of the cruise ship company.

Good old JJ came through at last. More likely, Unkie threatened to sue the shit out of them. This hotel they put us up in is top-notch. For three days they've treated us like regular VIPs. New clothes, food, unlimited bar tab, spa treatments. It sure made waiting for the trip home a little easier.

Tom started to doze off when someone knocked on the door. "Mr. Frye, it's the police."

Groggy, Tom got out of bed and answered the door to the police chief he'd met during his initial interrogation. "Uh hello, Chief."

"Sorry to disturb you, sir. But it's time for your exit interview with the Mayor. Can you get dressed and be ready to leave the hotel in a half-hour?"

"Sure."

"Very well, sir. We will wait for you in the lobby."

"Great. Thanks."

This is fantastic! A few days earlier than we hoped. This should make Mina happy. He jumped into the shower and then changed into one of the new pairs of pants and shirts the concierge had brought up to him earlier. He packed the rest of his complimentary clothes and toiletries into the small suitcase they'd given him and met the police downstairs.

Mina sat in one of the overstuffed hotel lobby chairs looking agitated. She drummed her newly manicured fingernails on the arm of the chair and threw him a dirty look.

"Oh, how nice of you to join us, Thomas."

"Nice to see you looking... cleaner."

Mina stood and stormed toward Tom. "You vile creature. How dare you?"

One of the police officers grabbed Mina's arm and redirected her. "Come *señora*, your police escort awaits."

"Let's go," the police chief said. "I'm sure you're anxious to leave."

Tom smiled and followed him out. "You have no idea."

***

Throngs of people crowded the streets all the way to the Mayor's office. They smiled and waved to the motorcade, jumping up and down, waving the flags of El Salvador and the United States. Children held balloons, sitting atop their father's shoulders.

194

"What is this?" Tom asked the police chief. "It looks like a parade."

"This *is* a parade, Mr. Frye. A celebration for you and Mrs. Stab. The people of Acajutla are happy you are both returned safely and the general is in custody."

"Wow. I'm shocked. I never expected this."

"Yes, well. You'll see our little city has some special things planned for you both today."

"What? For us?"

"Mr. Frye, when you texted your wife from the MS 13 compound with the doctor's phone, and she relayed the information to the United States authorities, we worked in conjunction with the Salvadoran Government. And then, after you made contact with international emergency responders that same day, agents were able to trace the signal from the phone, and then eventually locate the general at the hospital where we arrested him."

"Arrested? The general? What about the doctor? And the priest?"

"The doctor was there merely as a humanitarian. He was never arrested. But the priest..."

"Wow. I can't believe it."

"Ah, look. We're almost to the Mayor's office at City Hall. He'll be waiting to greet you."

"Thank God, Mina is in a separate car. I hope we get to the Mayor first."

The police chief laughed. "Yes. We thought it best to separate you two."

Tom smiled and nodded in agreement. "Good thinking."

"Here we are at City Hall. And there is Mayor Lopez now."

A chubby man wearing a black suit smiled and waved. Around his neck he wore several medals hanging from thick silk sashes. He opened the car door and greeted Tom and the chief, shaking hands and smiling.

"Welcome, Mr. Frye. Thank you for coming. And where is Mrs. Stab?"

"They're pulling in behind us now," the chief said. The second police car parked, and Mina stepped out.

The mayor and the police chief escorted Tom and Mina to a large stage erected in the City Hall parking lot. The massive crowd, which spread as far as Tom could see, cheered and clapped as they took the stage. Tom saw news crews flanking the crowd. Photographers snapped photos and television journalists reported the event live. Some of the most aggressive reporters shouted questions as they walked past. *I can't believe this is all for us. Holy shit. God, I hope Vicky and the girls are watching.*

Mayor Lopez opened his speech by welcoming the guests of honor. He spoke in English, while a petite woman at the end of the stage translated into Spanish.

"Friends, please join me in welcoming our special guests of honor for this celebration today—Mr. Thomas Frye and Mrs. Mina Stab, the Americans who had been held hostage at the MS 13 headquarters by General Garcia and his soldiers."

The crowd cheered, but some among them shouted taunts and jeers about the general. Mayor Lopez motioned for the crowd to settle down before he continued his speech.

"My good people of Acajutla. I have the honor of sharing wonderful news with you and all of our friends watching on television." He spread his hands out and nodded to the media presence. "First of all, Mr. Frye and Mrs. Stab, I want to tell you that General Garcia and some of his top advisors are currently detained in a Panamanian prison. They are charged with kidnapping, murder, human trafficking, drug smuggling, extortion and rape. More charges will likely follow."

The crowd went wild, screaming and cheering. The mayor continued his speech when they settled down. "For many years, El Salvador has suffered under MS 13's corruption and violence, and it is largely because of your involvement, Mr. Frye and Mrs. Stab, that they are behind bars today." Loud applause erupted from the crowd again, and the mayor let it continue.

Shocked and surprised, Tom and Mina looked at each other.

"How? How did this happen?" Mina asked the mayor while they waited for the crowd to quiet.

The mayor raised his hand and the crowd hushed again. "Citizens of Acajutla, Mrs. Stab and Mr. Frye asked how this could be true? I will tell you." He paused for a moment before continuing. "When General Garcia and his henchmen took the girl Lupe and baby Thomasina Mina to the hospital, they were ambushed by the Panamanian police, who arrested the general and his men. A tip had been called in anonymously and the authorities intercepted them as Lupe processed through registration." More cheers broke out in the crowd. "The Salvadoran police have closed the MS 13 camp and arrested everyone supporting the general's corrupt work. All those imprisoned against their will, and the women and children who were forced to remain there, have been relocated."

"My God," Tom said. "I can't believe it."

"What about the baby? And Lupe?" Mina asked.

"They are well," the mayor said and then repeated for the crowd, "Lupe and the baby are out of the hospital and staying with relatives in Panama for now. After the police spoke with her, Lupe agreed to file rape charges against General Garcia. Their relationship was not consensual."

"This is not the outcome I expected," Tom said.

"Well, of course not. You create trouble wherever you go, Thomas," Mina said.

"Enough, please," the Chief of Police cut Mina off. "Let the mayor finish."

The mayor continued, "So Tom Frye and Mina Stab, the citizens of Acajutla and all of El Salvador thank you for your bravery and your help in arresting the notorious General Garcia, head of MS 13." The crowd clapped. "And in honor of your service, we would like to give you both keys to our city." The mayor beckoned to a young boy and girl who presented

Tom and Mina with oversized keys. A blue bow decorated Tom's key, and a pink bow fluttered on Mina's.

"In addition," the mayor continued, "Tom Frye, as of this day, you are an honorary Mayor of Acajutla." Tom bowed his head in embarrassment, his cheeks turning pink with the attention. Everyone cheered except Mina. "Your brave actions in the prison camp alerted the authorities, allowing them to track the general."

"Brave actions? What brave actions?" Mina said.

"During your captivity, Mr. Frye was able to smuggle the doctor's cell phone into the bathroom and send a text message to his wife. Mrs. Frye contacted the authorities, who were able to trace the call and follow the GPS from the doctor's cell phone, which ultimately led to the arrest of the general and his henchmen."

Mina looked at Tom, shocked and in disbelief. "You never told me this!"

"I never knew if the text went through," Tom said. "After I sent it, I had to delete the conversation from the doctor's phone. And then, the call to 112—the International Emergency Number. I thought that was a real stretch. I didn't know how much they understood." He looked at Mina and shrugged. "Shortly after, they released us, and I didn't know if it made any difference."

"Well, goodie for you. But Honorary Mayor of Acajutla? What about me? I delivered the baby."

The media snapped to attention, turning their focus on Mina and her outburst. The crowed hummed. Cameras clicked and snapped.

"Ah, Mrs. Mina Stab," the mayor said as he addressed her and the murmuring crowd, "for you we have a special honor."

"Special honor? Well that's more like it. What is it?"

"We have decided to change the name of our little craft market from the Maximiliano Hernandez Martinez Craft Market to the Mina Stab Wildlife Bird Sanctuary and Craft

Market. People will gather here to look at our Bird Sanctuary and be able to buy souvenirs. Isn't that wonderful?"

"Indeed," Mina huffed, looking annoyed. "When do we get out of this horrid place? I've never been so insulted in my life. Bird sanctuary..."

As Tom and Mina posed for pictures with the mayor and police, the crowd grew silent. In the distance, a helicopter came into view and moved in their direction. As it got closer, Tom saw the American flag emblazoned beside the words United States Coast Guard. The helicopter continued to descend, and police cleared the crowd and flagged the helicopter to land in a field behind the building.

"What's happening?" Tom asked the mayor. "Is that for us?"

"It is, Mr. Frye. That helicopter is here to take you to a Coast Guard aircraft, waiting for you at the airport in San Salvador. From there, they will fly you to your families in California."

Tom grabbed Mina and hugged her, lifting her off her feet.

She slapped him and struggled out of his grasp. "Put me down, you idiot. What's wrong with you?"

Tom waved goodbye to the cheering crowd and even Mina offered a limp wave. The police escorted them off the stage and they made their way to the helicopter. Reporters chased after them, firing questions, begging for comments before they boarded.

Mina pushed Tom out of the way and climbed in the chopper first. A pretty blonde reporter tugged on Tom's shirt sleeve as he waited his turn, calling out in a heavily accented voice, "Excuse, please. *Señor* Frye, will you finish the rest of your vacation? Your cruise that was interrupted? Maybe come back to El Salvador again?"

Tom smiled and spoke into the microphone. "Travel? No. I don't think I'll be traveling for a long time."

The reporter looked puzzled. "No?"

Tom waved goodbye to the crowd and moved to board the chopper. "No, *señorita. No me gusta. Adios, El Salvador.*"

EPILOGUE

Tom adjusted the collar of his jacket and pulled on a knit cap retrieved from his pocket. Although technically Spring, the howling March winds bit into his bones, engulfing his entire body with the aches and pains of late middle age. Light snow fell, landing on his eyelashes, and leaving a dusty trail across the parking lot and fields.

He called out to Walter, working across the lot, "Hey, I'm getting too old for this shit."

"Eh, don't tell me you're getting soft on me, boss?"

"I am, Walt. Right now, all I can think about is some hot soup for lunch, a couple of Advil and a stiff drink tonight when I get home."

"Call it a day, Tom. I can finish cleaning up the lot for our delivery next week."

"I think I will. Thanks." Tom gathered his tools and returned them to the shed. He stamped his feet at the Bumpkin's entrance, shaking the snow out of his hat and gloves and tossing them on the bench inside. The dreary weather, devoid of sun, depressed him, making him think about the cruise vacation-turned-disaster two months before.

Inside, he spotted Vicky working on the new Spring displays with Heather, the Assistant Manager. They giggled and plotted designs for the store, oblivious to the weather outside. Vicky, the quintessential planner, thrived in her role at the Bumpkin. He smiled, proud of how far she'd come these past few years in this business. In several weeks, he realized, Easter would be here, and Jane and Sophie would be home for Spring break. He looked forward to spending some quality family time. Now more than ever, he needed them.

As Tom reviewed the huge order of seasonal flowers and plants scheduled to arrive the next week, his mind raced. He worried the weather could stay frigid and the tender plants would be defenseless against Mother Nature. *Huh, I'd thought the stock market could be unpredictable, but it's nothing compared to the weather. Ironic.*

"Oh well, it's time for my lunch." He rummaged in the office refrigerator until he found the container of vegetable soup from home. *I'm so glad I married a woman who can cook.* No sooner had he put the soup in the microwave, when the door buzzer alerted him. *Customer? That's strange.*

"Yoo hoo," a familiar voice called. "Anybody home?"

"Peggy?" Tom walked out of his office to find his former secretary shaking the snow from her coat.

"Hi, Tom."

"What in the hell brings you out on such a miserable day?"

"Hello to you, too. Nice manners."

"Uh, sorry. I'm just surprised to see you. We don't have any new seasonal stuff in stock yet. Technically, we're not even open for business."

"Well, then you should look your door if you're not open. Jeez Louise. I mean, if you don't want people coming in, then—"

Tom straightened up and interrupted, "Peggy. Hello. What brings you in today?"

"I guess you haven't heard, huh?"

"Heard what?"

"About Lance."

"What about Lance?" *Jesus can this woman never get to the point?*

"See, this is what I meant. I figured you hadn't heard, and well—news like this should be delivered in person. I mean—"

"Peggy! For God's sake. What about Lance? Is he dead?"

"Oh no. Nothing like that. I mean, it's bad. But not that bad. You see he—"

Tom interrupted, firmly steering her to the pair of chairs in his office. "Peggy. Let's sit. Here." She nodded and plopped down across from him. "Tell me what happened."

Peggy took a deep breath. "He's in the psych ward. At Cray Community Hospital."

"What? What happened?"

"He had a complete mental breakdown. Came into the office on Monday wearing that old mechanic's jumpsuit he wears when he's working on his antique car. You know, the one that's all greasy and filthy that he's always wearing in his Facebook pictures?"

Tom couldn't help grinning. "Well, that's pretty bad. But not bad enough to get committed."

"Well, duh. If you'd stop interrupting me, I could finish my story. Jeez Louise."

Stifling a laugh, Tom made a zipping motion across his lips.

"So, as I was saying, he came in filthy, wearing that awful jumpsuit. And Frank, the big boss happened to be in the office. He flipped out because clients were in the building. Told Lance to get out of that getup immediately." Peggy blew a huge bubble with her gum and popped it. "So, he did."

"You've lost me. So, he changed into one of the suits he keeps at work? So what?"

"No! He stripped down. Buck naked and walked around the office. Went to get coffee in the breakroom, and asked one of the admins to make copies for him."

"Naked?"

"Naked as a jaybird. It was disgusting." Peggy shuddered.

"So, what happened next?"

"Lance refused to get dressed. Claimed he was tired of people criticizing his clothes, so he'd work naked from now on. The police arrested him for indecent exposure. When they called his wife, she suggested they commit him." Peggy's eyes widened. "Evidently, he'd been refusing to wear clothes at home, too, and the neighbors filed a formal complaint with the police a couple of weeks ago."

"Unbelievable. So now what?"

"Word is, he'll be forced to retire. And we're in a tight spot, Tom."

"Whaddaya mean?"

"Frank asked me to come talk to you. He asked if you kept your licenses active—the CFP, Insurance, Series Seven, you know. I told him I thought so." Peggy paused and looked into his eyes. "Tom. They want you to come back."

***

Tom marveled at the difference a couple of weeks had made. The weather had turned seasonably warm, and the sunshine on his face made him smile. He proudly surveyed the Spring inventory, expertly displayed by his competent staff. Walter's talent and years of experience showed in every inch of the Country Bumpkin. Tom couldn't wait to tell him the news. And then he thought about Vicky.

He walked into the store and watched his wife tidying the front end. She swept and tossed some empty boxes into the recycling bin. "Hi, honey." Vicky smiled and waved. "Ready to go home?"

"Yep, it's that time. We're the last ones here. As usual."

"No. I think Walter is roaming around somewhere. I saw his truck in the parking lot when I took out the trash a minute ago."

"No doubt." Tom walked over to Vicky and wrapped her into a big hug.

"Wow. What was that for?"

"Vick, it's such a nice night. Let's go outside and sit on the bench for a minute before we go home."

"Sure, sounds good."

Together they locked up everything then Tom grabbed two bottles of beer from the tiny fridge in his office. "Join me in a beverage?" he asked with a sheepish grin.

"Ooh sure, why not? I haven't had a beer in ages. What's the occasion?"

When they'd sat down outside the store, Tom popped opened the beer and they clinked their bottles together. For a few minutes they sipped in silence, but Vicky prompted Tom again. "So? What's up?"

"I think it's time to change things up around here. Move forward with a new plan."

"Excuse me? What do you mean 'new plan'?"

"Vick, you knew that since Lance's breakdown, I've been in communication with Global Financial again, right? Particularly with the big boss, Frank?"

"Yeah. So?" Vicky's forehead creased intuitively.

"They've made me an offer I can't refuse. Literally." Tom laughed nervously. "They're desperate. With Lance on disability, Frank needs help. He's offered me the chance to work part-time. With a select group of clients that I can cherry pick with his blessing."

"Go back there? But what about the Country Bumpkin?"

"I've been thinking. We maintain ownership of the Bumpkin. Let Walter run things. You can stay on in your role— I mean, if you want to. My hours will be more flexible, and with fewer clients I'll be able to manage." Vicky continued to stare at Tom, dumbfounded. "Walter can handle it. We both know that."

Vicky's face relaxed slightly, but she looked uneasy. "Tom. Is this really what you want?"

"Yes. This is it, Vick. The perfect balance."

She put her bottle of beer on the ground and took his hand. "Tom Frye, I don't know what I'm going to do with you."

"Do this with me, Vick. I can't do it without you on board."

"Okay. We'll give it a whirl. But promise me. If things get bad again, you'll give it up."

Tom held up his hand in the Boy Scout pledge. "I promise."

"Okay, I guess we should go tell Walter about his promotion?"

"Great." They tossed their empty bottles in the recycling bin and set off to look for Walter. "He must be at the Christmas Tree farm. He mentioned going out there before he left today to flag some of the trees for trimming.

Together they hiked up the path to the tree farm when Tom stopped in his tracks. "Did you hear that?"

"What?" Vicky asked, oblivious.

"That sound."

"I don't hear a thing, Tom. Hurry up, I want to get out of here before dark."

They continued walking when a flash of black emerged from a lush dwarf white pine near the path. Then they both heard it. Mewling. Shocked, they looked at each other. Cautiously they proceeded toward the sounds.

"Oh, no." Tom pointed. Standing guard in front of the pine stood a large, black cat.

"Tom, is that Kitty?"

Tom edged a bit closer and the cat met him halfway. He looked closely, kneeling to get a better look. The animal came up to Tom and circled around his legs, purring. No collar. This must be the other cat. The nice one. He bent down and petted it, mesmerized.

"God. Be careful, Tom." Vicky approached more tentatively.

"Yeah, well at least now you believe me. There were two cats. This is the one without the collar I told you about." Tom tried to walk away, but the cat continued to twine around his ankles. "This is weird. I don't think it wants me to leave. Like, it's trying to tell me something." The cat moved away, ducking into the pine, but then emerged again. A feline game of hide and seek. "I want to see what's in the bush."

"Tom, no. Let's go."

But he ignored his wife and followed the cat. Bending over, he couldn't believe what he saw deep under the pine. The glint of her tag sparkled against her black fur. Kitty! And a new litter of kittens. "Vick! Come see. It's Kitty, and more kittens."

"Oh my gosh, I don't believe it. I guess your other black cat must be the father. Mister Kitty, the proud papa."

Tom smiled. "Well done, Mr. Kitty. Congrats on your new family."

"Tom. Don't you dare touch the mother cat. Remember what happened last time?"

Tom stopped, facing his wife. "Please, Vick. I never make the same mistake twice."

Laughing, hand in hand, they left the feline family to themselves and walked up the hill to find Walter.

The End

ABOUT THE AUTHOR

A graduate of The Pennsylvania State University with a Bachelor's Degree in Communications, Arts and Sciences and a Minor in English, SANDRA M. BUSH has a background in Federal, State and County Government.

In 2014 she decided to pursue freelance writing opportunities. She has published articles in the Pennsylvania School Board Association's magazine *The Bulletin*, and the online magazine *Keystone Edge* as well as work in advertising, and museum script writing for the Oil Heritage Museum, Titusville, PA.

Currently Sandy is the Area 5 Representative for Pennwriters, an organization dedicated to assisting writers of all levels and genres.

Sandy lives with her husband Todd in Pennsylvania. They are the parents of daughters Chelsea and Monica and pet parents to cats Gracie and Boo.

Visit her blog, *Sandy's Snarky Snippets*:
www.sandrambush.com

ALSO BY SANDRA M. BUSH

Money Man (Book 1)
Tom Frye's life couldn't get much better. The handsome financial advisor has a lucrative career, a beautiful family and a McMansion on the golf course. But when his wacky, demanding clients push him to the brink of madness, he turns to unhealthy methods of coping.

Can he find a way to turn his life around that doesn't involve Valium, Heineken or Swedish Fish?

Fans of John Irving and Wally Lamb will appreciate this dark comedic spin on one man's journey to find a new career without losing his mind, his family or his dignity.

Made in the USA
Lexington, KY
30 October 2019